HIS NEW TOY

(Forced Feminization Stories)

Jane Doe

Contents

Chapter 1 3
Chapter 2 8
Chapter 3 13
Chapter 4 17
Chapter 5 22
Chapter 6 28
Chapter 7 32
Chapter 8 39
Chapter 9 41
Chapter 10 46
Chapter 11 50
Chapter 12 55
Chapter 13 59
Chapter 14 64
Chapter 15 67
Epilogue 74

CHAPTER 1

Trying to find a lover in the times of Covid has been a nightmare, not that I had much luck before Covid. I guess being a closet crossdresser who's not sure what you're looking for in a lover doesn't make it any easier to find a suitable partner. I've scoured all of the dating sites and tried a few out, but I'm always left with the same result. I have been disappointed and left wondering, is there really anyone out there for me?

About a month ago, I went on tinder and found a match with a girl that I used to go to school with. Our chatting about our alma mater lasted until the bread came, from there it was a painful exercise trying to find something we both enjoyed talking about.
"How do you like your job?" I asked, trying to pretend to be interested.
"Oh you know, it pays the bills. Did you say you're in marketing?" She asked back, pretending to be enthused.
"Yeah, we just started a new campaign targeting the elderly today."
"Oh that's exciting…"
"Yeah, super exciting…"
I wanted to leave before the meal came, but I felt some semblance of responsibility to pay the bill and decided to stick it out to the end.

Between awkward meetups, and an increasing number of girls that just didn't want to risk getting together with a stranger, my desire for companionship was starting to feel hopeless. Did I even deserve a good girl? After all, I wasn't really looking to be the chivalrous prince charming who swept a girl off of her feet. A part of me deep down wanted to be that girl and get swept off of my feet by my own prince charming. I told myself I wanted a girl who was ok with crossdressing and who would indulge my kinky desires, but I was starting to wonder if that really was what I wanted.

Before I looked for a mate and possibly settled into a life I thought I wanted, I thought that maybe I owed it to myself to fully explore my desires and see what I might be missing out on. I had read stories and fantasized for years about things like "forced feminization" and "sissy maids", but what would it be like to actually indulge whole heartedly for once? These were the thoughts that lead me down a rabbit hole I could never return from.

After getting bored with my usual google searches, I decided to hop on Craig's list and try looking for someone interested in a curious crossdresser. Within a thirty minutes, I found a match. It almost sounded like a fantasy as I read the ad to myself, 'I am a businessman who is looking for a sissy that I can dominate. I am looking for a full time partner who is willing to listen to my every command and isn't afraid of full feminization.' I was hard just reading the ad.

I was weary of the post, but couldn't resist replying with my phone number. I felt like I owed myself to at least try. About a half hour later, I received a text on my phone.

"Hi, this is Conner Wellington, I saw you responded to my post."

I texted back, "Yes, I am definitely interested, but I didn't see very much information on what you're looking for?"

"I like to be careful what I put on the internet. I am looking for someone who will live in my penthouse with me, clean up, and just make sure they look pretty for me when I get home."

I was leaking in my panties as I read the text message coming through. This was like a dream come true. I could live with someone who would not only let me crossdress, but encourage it daily. I had to find out what the catch was.

"So is there anything else, am I missing something?" I asked.

"I just want a sissy who will listen to me and devote all of her attention to me. You can't have your own apartment, you won't need to work. You just need to focus on making yourself as feminine as possible for me."

My stomach fluttered with butterflies as I read his text. This was everything I had ever fantasized about presenting itself on a silver platter. My fingers jittered as I typed back, "When can I start?"

Conner invited me over to his penthouse for a preliminary meeting. He made sure to tell me that I should come in my regular male clothes and that everything I would ever need would be provided. I listened to his orders and came dressed in my jeans and long sleeve shirt.

A taxi dropped me off at the address that Conner provided. As I arrived, I realized we were in the heart of the city and that Conner's building was the fourth tallest. Multiple workers were stationed at the entrance of the skyscraper and were aware of who I was before I arrived. I was greeted and escorted to the elevator at the back of the main entrance.

After a surprisingly short ride to the 25th floor, the elevator opened up directly to Conner's penthouse. I was in awe as I exited the elevator and took in the illustrious suite. Filled with astonishment, I took in the crown molding, priceless works of art sprinkled on the walls, and only the highest quality of plush furniture. I felt completely out of place as Conner walked toward me wearing a blazer and black dress pants. He was confident in his body and wasn't concerned he didn't have a shirt on under his blazer.

"Hello, you must be Ray." He said walking toward me with his hand extended.

"Yes, and you must be Conner Wellington." I said meeting his hand and shaking it.

"You can address me as Conner."

"Oh, I'm sorry, Conner."

"Don't worry about it. It's very nice to meet you. To be honest, I'm just glad you didn't turn out to be another bot."

"Oh my god right, I was thinking the same thing. It all sounded too good to be true."

"Well, we'll see if you still think that after we discuss a few things. Why don't you join me in the dining room."

Conner turned and started walking down the hall. He expected me to follow him down the hall to the last door on the right, so I did.

As we stepped into the dining room, I noticed floor to ceiling windows that overlooked the river running through and out of the city. With the late afternoon upon us, the sun reflected off of the river and gave it a shimmering glow. Conner lowered some shades with a remote control as he sat at the head of the table and gestured for me to sit next to him. I followed his order and took a seat.

"So, I'm sure you have lots of questions and I have a few things I would like to discuss, so let's just get started. You are comfortable with wearing an array of women's clothing, correct?"

I could feel butterflies in my stomach as I answered him, "Yes, I...I do like to crossdress."

"And do you have any problems giving up your residence and living here full time?"

"I guess not? What will I do with all of my stuff though?"

"I don't want any remnants of your old life here. All of your things will be disposed of by my people and you will begin living here tonight. However, I will reimburse you fifty thousand dollars as compensation." My eyes went wide as I sat back in my chair and took in his offer.

I rented my apartment and filled it with old pieces of furniture that relatives had donated to me over the years. I did have a new TV and various electronic devices, but there was no way all of it would amount to anything close to fifty thousand dollars. Although it made sense monetarily, I still didn't know how I felt about throwing everything away. I felt anxiety creeping up as I gave my answer to Conner who was staring patiently with his piercing blue eyes.

"Yeah ok. I'm...I'll be ok starting now."

"Lastly, what, if any, are your limits to feminizing yourself? I want you to be honest with me here because I will push you to your limits."

I looked up and left as I thought about his question. I read hundreds of stories about sissies being humiliated, tied up, forced to give blow jobs, and completely at the mercy of another. I was obsessed with giant breasts and had imagined what it would be like to have my own pair for years. Although I never thought about actually going through with a surgery, I wasn't sure if I wanted to rule it out?

"I don't think I have any limits?" I answered.

Conner tilted his head as he stared at me. I could feel him trying to figure me out as we sat in the dining room. After a few moments, Conner smiled politely. Apparently he felt like he had seen enough and congratulated me.

"Well Ray, I like what I see and hear. Congratulations, let me show you to your room."

I felt a wave of relief and excitement as he stood up from the table and gestured for me to follow him.

We walked down the hall before stopping at one of the large dark wooden doors. He opened the door and showed me inside the guest bedroom. Large glass windows overlooked the city from the opposite side of the dining room. A private bathroom was attached as well as a large walk in closet. I walked inside the room and stood next next to a king bed made up with the softest of pink sheets.

"There should be plenty of outfits in the closet for you to choose from. Dispose of your clothes and get dressed in any of the outfits you choose. We'll eat dinner in two hours so that should give you enough time for your makeup."

"Yes sir." I said with giddiness.

Conner left the room after closing the door.

CHAPTER 2

I stood in the closet of my new room, dazzled by how many clothes were in front of me. I couldn't believe how many dresses, skirts, and high heels were neatly organized for me to choose from. I didn't make that much money and had been previously limited to the few women's outfits and high heels I could afford. But, those days were over.

I ran my fingers through the dresses hanging on the rack. I loved the soft smooth feelings from the long flowing gowns and skirts hanging side by side. I couldn't resist any longer and decided to try something on.

I found a long red dress with a zipper running up the back that called out to me. I pulled it from the hanger and held it against my body. It looked like it would be a close fit. I stripped myself of my male clothes and tossed them in the garbage before stepping into the dress and pulling it up. The smooth soft fabric sent shivers up me as I pulled it over my shoulders. I had become quite proficient at zipping the back of my dresses and had no problem reaching behind me. But, I quickly noticed that I was having a hard time zipping this dress all the way to the top. I sucked in my gut and tugged as I jumped around my room. After much effort, I managed to get the zipper to the top. I walked over to the full length mirror hanging on my closet door and checked myself out.

The long red dress was at floor length with a split running up my right leg. The long silky material draped across my body and felt softer then anything that I had previously worn. The dress came in around my waist and looked like it was at its limit as it pressed against me. Around my chest it was another story. I had absolutely no chest and this dress flowed out so that it could fit someone with at least a DD cup.

I shrugged my shoulders and reached behind me for the zipper. Pulling it down was much easier than pulling it up as I had the dress stripped off and hung back up in a few moments. As I stood naked in front of the mirror, I realized just how manly I still looked. If I was going to make a good first impression for my new master, I needed to prep myself.

I walked into the bathroom and turned on the shower. It was done with tan stones and had inlaid shelves stocked with Nair, shaving cream, and a fresh razor. I looked at the vanity in front of the mirror and saw make up spread out across the countertop. There were foundations for every skin tone, different types of eyeliner pencils and markers, eye shadows in an array of colors, various mascaras, powders, blushes, bronzers, eyebrow pencils, lip glosses, lipsticks in every color, and lip liners to match any of my choices. I felt like I was living out a dream as I stared at everything in the bathroom for me to use.

I felt overwhelmed looking over everything this man had just provided for me. I couldn't believe that some person I didn't know was willing to let me live out my fantasies and not ask me for any money. I pinched myself to make sure I wasn't dreaming.

I stepped into the shower and decided to start with the nair. I had used it a few times before and liked the results. I rubbed it over most of my body and waited a few minutes before washing it off. Just like my last use, all of my body hair started falling right off. I had shaved my body semi frequently, but I always enjoyed the feeling of fresh smooth skin. I grabbed the razor and did a quick once over myself to make sure I had gotten everything off.

Once I finished removing all of my body hair, I stepped out of the shower and dried myself with a white fluffy towel hanging on the rack. Even the towels felt luxurious in this penthouse. I dabbed myself off and wiped the mirror from the steam that had built up. I checked my face and double checked that all of my body hair was removed except for my shoulder length hair on top of my head.

After tying my hair back in a pony tail, I began looking through the foundations to try and find my color. Holding a couple bottles to my face, I found a nice light tube that complimented my skin. I grabbed a brush and blotted some foundation on before spreading it across my face. I made sure to spread it thin before adding any more foundation to my brush. I went over every inch of my face and made sure it was perfect.

Once finished with the liquid foundation, I grabbed the setting powder and began applying it. I went over every inch of my face again and made sure that both layers would stay in place. I wanted to do my best for my first meeting with Conner en Fem.

I began applying bronzer and lighter powders to try and create a contour around my nose, cheek bones, and jaw. It had taken some work for me to learn the techniques, but over time I started to feel more comfortable trying more difficult makeup applications.

Once I felt like I had done enough contouring, I found a black out eye liner pencil and began circling my eyes. I had a shaky hand and always struggled to keep the line thin. After doing the best I was able, I took a closer look in the mirror again. "It's not perfect, but I'll never finish if that's my goal." I said to myself while shrugging.

I grabbed some dark eye shadow and began applying it to my eyes for a smokey look. I felt more confident in this area as I replicated what I had seen in some YouTube videos on each eye. It didn't take long before my brown eyes started to pop behind all of the dark eye makeup.

I finished my eyes with a full application of extra volume mascara. I felt like my lashes were the longest I had ever seen as I spent a few minutes on each eye, blinking against the wand with my mouth slightly open.

After staring at my mouth in the mirror, I started looking down and thinking about what lipstick and lip liner to use. I pulled out a few different red tubes, but decided to go with the darkest red available. I used a slightly lighter lip liner to outline my cupid's arrow as well as the rest of my lips. Once I went around my lips ever so slowly with the lip liner, I filled between the lines with my lipstick.

I always loved staring at myself in the mirror after finishing my makeup. I hardly recognized the person in the mirror staring back at me. My eyes were dark and alluring while my lips screamed for something to slide between them. I felt as sexy as I had ever been. The only thing left before dressing was my hair.

I had enjoyed crossdressing for years and decided to grow out my hair to a feminine length over two years ago. It was finally down to my shoulders in slight waves, but I hadn't spent much time styling it. I owned a long straight blonde wig and preferred wearing that when crossdressing. But without my wig, I needed to figure something out.

I started by letting my hair down from the ponytail and brushing it out. I fought through a plethora of knots as I tried to remember the last time I had brushed it. After a few minutes of struggling with my hair, the brush started moving through it easily. Looking through the drawers under the sink, I found a straightener and plugged it in. I hadn't had much experience with a hair straightener, but I managed to remove the waves without burning myself. With the long straight brown hair and a full face of makeup, I was starting to match how I felt. Now, it was time for my favorite part, getting dressed.

I walked to the dresser and began pulling out the drawers. Neatly folded and separated into their own drawers, I found a wide variety of panties and bras. My middle started pointing straight into the air as I looked through all of my options. My eyes landed on a matching pink set of panties and bra in front of me. I pulled out the panties and slipped them on over my rock hard member. They fit very snugly. I slid my arms through the bra and pulled the strap behind me. After fastening the bra, I stepped in front of the mirror hanging on the closet door.

My panties felt a little tight while my bra looked completely empty. It was clear this bra was meant for someone with a set of E cups while I was lucky to fill out an A. Not seeing anything smaller, I shrugged my shoulders and went to the closet to find a dress.

I spent a few minutes looking through my options again and tried to imagine what my host would like to see. He displayed an elegant mixture of classiness and sexiness. I wanted to do my best to match his style. I found a short black long sleeve dress that seemed to fit what I was looking for. I pulled it off the hanger and began sliding into it.

I felt the same problem with this dress as I did with the last one as I pulled at the zipper. It took me a few minutes, but with some struggling, I managed to zip it up to my neck. I walked over to the mirror and checked my reflection. I felt like I had to keep my gut sucked in as the dress pulled tightly around my waist. The dress came down to my upper thigh and definitely gave a sexy appeal. The padding in the bra somewhat filled out the chest, but it looked like there was still plenty of room. The top of the dress came up to my neck and felt like it gave me some modesty, despite showing most of my legs. I looked down to my feet and smiled before picking out my last item.

I walked to the back of the closet where small shoe holes filled up the entire wall. There were high heels and only high heels in a wide selection of styles and colors. None of the shoes or boots were less than four inches in height while many were much taller. I loved high heels and felt like I was in heaven as I looked through the pairs of pumps, sandals, and wedges. However, I found myself gravitating toward a pair of black five inch strappy sandal heels. I grabbed the pair from the shoe hole and sat on my bed as I put them on.

There were multiple straps that came up around my ankle and wrapped around twice. I made sure to pull them tight before fastening each heel on my feet. I stood up from the bed and strutted over to the mirror. I felt like a real woman as I took in the image in the mirror.

Elegant and sexy high heels lead up to my soft and smooth legs. My dress at my upper thighs begged for attention while still leaving the imagination to work. The tightness around my waist and the padding in my bra gave a slight hourglass figure. My lips were a deep dark red and my eyes popped behind the dark eye makeup. I was ready to show myself to Conner.

I looked at the clock and saw that I managed to get ready twenty minutes early. I decided to take the time to explore the penthouse and see what Conner was up to. I stepped over to the door and grabbed the handle. To my surprise, it was locked.

I pulled at the handle and jiggled it, but it wouldn't move. I began getting nervous and knocking on the door. I never met this man, and now I was locked in one of his bedrooms, dressed en fem from head to toe. I couldn't hear anyone in the hallway and started to pace back and forth in my room. Where the hell could Conner be?

CHAPTER 3

After a nervous twenty minutes pacing around my room, I finally heard footsteps walking toward my door. I stopped next to the window and stood facing the door as I saw the handle turning. The door opened to reveal a butler standing in the doorway.
"Good evening madam, would you please follow me." The butler said.
I had a million questions for him, like who are you and why did you lock me in here? But, I decided to follow behind him and not make a problem yet.

Following the butler down the hall, I observed that he was wearing an all black suit and white gloves. He walked with one arm behind his back and his other arm stiff in front of him. I was mesmerized with his mannerisms as we came to the dining room door and stopped. The butler opened the door and stood against it while gesturing for me to walk inside.

My heart was pounding as I stood beside the door. This was my first night and first appearance as a sissy for Conner. I had so many thoughts floating through my head about my own self worth. 'Would if he doesn't like me? Would if he thinks I'm not cute enough? Would if I'm not what he's looking for?' I felt anxiety creeping up as the butler gestured for me to step inside again. I took a deep breath before walking in.

I felt a wave of relief and confusion as I saw an empty table. The butler walked over to the table and gestured for me to sit where I had earlier next to Conner. I followed his instruction and took my seat as the butler pushed in my chair behind me. The butler stepped back to the wall and froze in place. I looked behind my chair and could see that he was staring straight ahead out the floor to ceiling windows on the other side of the dining room table. I turned back around and looked out the window as well.

The glow of the sun was disappearing on the horizon. The trees and river were still just barely visible in the twilight before us. I smiled as I took in the beauty in front of me while seated at the fanciest table I had ever seen.

I heard footsteps down the hall before the butler stepped away from the wall and grabbed the door knob. On queue, the butler opened the door and bowed as Conner came bursting through. I didn't know whether to stand or stay seated and ended up halfway between the two as Conner marched over to the table and sat at his seat at the head. He paid no attention to me as he sat down and snapped his fingers, giving the signal for the butler to begin our meal. The butler scurried out of the room and began grabbing our first course of food. Conner pulled out his phone and began typing as we sat in silence.

I was so nervous, I didn't say anything as I waited for the butler to return. I timidly looked over at Conner and hoped that he would break the silence first. I hadn't gone out in public while crossdressed often and had no idea how to act around this new man. I glanced over at him before bringing my gaze back to the window. I shifted my eyes back and forth a few more times hoping he would notice me. After a few minutes of typing, he put his phone down and directed his full attention to me.

Looking at me with his deep, blue eyes, I began to feel butterflies fluttering in my stomach again. He remained silent as his eyes scanned my face and hair. He raised his eyebrows as his eyes continued glazing over my chest and stomach. His eyes stopped and lingered at the end of my dress where my thighs were bare. I swallowed my saliva as I felt this man meticulously observing my body.

"Well, you certainly do wear women's clothes." Conner observed.

"Thank you?" I said, not sure how to take his comment.

"The dress seems a little loose and tight at the same time."

"Yeah, I was just glad I was able to slide into it."

"And did the panties and bra fit alright?"

"Yeah, the bra felt a little loose though and the panties were a bit tight, but it's ok."

"Don't worry, we'll take care of that right away."

"May I ask what I'm supposed to do here?" I said nervously.

"What do you mean?" He asked.

"Well, my door was locked and I wasn't sure if you're expecting me to stay there all the time?"

"Oh. That is just a precaution for now. As I learn more about you and you gain my trust, that will change. I hope you understand."

"Yeah I guess that makes sense, I was just nervous being locked in a room by someone I just met, you know."

"Well, you should get used to it. You listen to me now."

I felt my stomach drop as he stared into my eyes. I could feel he was being entirely straight forward with me and I wasn't sure how to take it. I was both excited and terrified that I was being taken under control by this wealthy man. The silence was interrupted by the butler who appeared with two salads.

He slid a bowl of fresh greens with balsamic dressing in front of Conner then myself. Conner pulled the butler in and whispered something in his ear before he walked back to the kitchen. I wanted to ask what that was about, but I held my curiosity back.

I did my best to remain elegant and ladylike as we ate our salads. I would usually only eat salad if it was loaded with Caesar dressing and croutons, but this was surprisingly tasty. I finished the bowl and sat eagerly for the next course.

The butler returned a few minutes later with a sizzling hot plate that he slid in front of Conner. The butler grabbed our plates and returned to the kitchen. My eyes widened as I gazed at and smelled the buttery filet on Conner's plate. It was accompanied by garlic mashed potatoes and buttery green beans. I sat eagerly as I waited for the butler to return with my plate, but it never came.

I watched as Conner devoured his plate in front of me while I sat empty handed. I finally worked up the courage to ask what was going on.

"Is my steak coming?" I asked.

"Your steak?" He asked back.

"Yeah or do I get something else?"

"You just did have something else."

"What do you mean? The salad?"

"Yeah?"

"But that was so small?"

"And your waist is so large."

I sat back in my seat at his comment. I had never been overweight in my life and still wasn't. I looked down at myself for a moment before turning back up to Conner.

"I'm not that large." I said back.

"Believe me, you're huge. You're going to be on a strict diet until you bring your waistline down a few inches. Then we'll see about introducing some protein like this."

"How much weight do you want me to lose?" I asked.

"Enough so that you actually fit into that dress you're wearing. It looks ridiculous in your current state."

First he commented on my weight that I never thought was a problem, now he said I looked ridiculous in my dress. I sat back in my chair and turned my eyes down and away from Conner as I crossed my arms over my chest.

"And that's another problem. Your breasts, where are they?"

"What do you mean?" I said back almost losing my voice.

"You don't have any boobs. You know that's going to be a problem right?"

I swallowed the saliva in my mouth, "What do you mean, like surgery?"

"Well not right away, but eventually. If we take a few inches off the waist, have someone teach you how to do your makeup, and put some boobs on that chest, you might actually pass for a pretty girl."

I was squirming in my chair as I listened to Conner critique my body. I had felt so confident in front of the mirror a moment ago, but now I was suddenly aware of how masculine I actually looked. I brought my arms tighter over my chest as I nervously looked away from Conner.

"Hey, don't take it so hard. We all need a little work sometimes. Do you know how long it takes to maintain this hair everyday?"

I brought my eyes back to Conner. The short hair atop his head was pushed up at the front in a small wave. Small stubble shadowed each side of Conner's face and met below his chin as well as above his plump lips.

"Here, go on and touch it." He said as he reached out and grabbed my hand. I was hesitant, but he pulled my hand to his face and began rubbing it up and down. I was shocked at how soft his facial hair felt against the back of my hand.

"You don't get hair like this on accident."

"No you don't." I agreed.

The butler returned to the dining room and picked up Conner's plate. Conner sat up from the table and held out his hand for me. I nervously looked away before taking his hand and allowing him to help me to my feet. He pulled me out of the dining room and walked me to the living room at the end of the hall.

CHAPTER 4

At the end of the hallway, it opened up to the living room which featured floor to ceiling windows on the back wall. Conner led me to the center of the windows and held my hips as he guided me directly in front of the glass. He pressed against my back and wrapped his hands around my waist as we gazed upon the city lights.

"It's beautiful isn't it?" Conner whispered.

"It's breath taking." I agreed.

"I love looking out here at night. Something about watching the busyness from up here is peaceful for me." Conner said as he leaned in closer to me. "But, it's much better enjoying it with someone."

I felt his breath against my neck as shivers ran down my back. I put my hand over Conner's hand on my hip before reaching my other hand up behind my head. My fingers ran through the stubble on his face as we gazed out on the city.

Anxiety consumed me as I stood with Conner directly behind me in his living room. I eagerly awaited his next move as I felt his middle press against my behind. As he pressed against my dress, I could feel that he was starting to grow in his pants. My stomach fluttered as I realized I must've been somewhat attractive to him.

Conner brought his hands up to my shoulders and turned me around in front of him. In my heels, the top of my head just barely reached his mouth. I bit my lip as he gazed into my eyes. He turned his head to the side then started putting pressure on my shoulders. I tried not to resist and slowly fell down to my knees in front of him.

My mouth began to salivate as I stared up at Conner from my knees. He brought his thumb to my lips and pushed it inside. As I looked up as him grinning at me, I began sucking his finger and moving my tongue around it. I tried to keep eye contact with him as I moved my head back and forth, trying to show what I was capable of. I closed my eyes as I continued and started to let out soft moans. I was starting to feel aroused before he pulled his hand back and stepped away.

"I better turn in for the night. You have a lovely evening." Conner said as he turned and walked away. My heart sank as I watched him walk down the hall. He opened the double doors to his bedroom and stepped inside.

I shook my head in disbelief as I sat on my knees a few moments longer. I couldn't help but think I had done something wrong for him to leave so abruptly. I started asking myself a myriad of questions as I stood up and walked back to my room.

'What just happened? I thought I had done a great job with my makeup and outfit choice. I shaved everything and felt like I couldn't have done anything more to present myself en fem for him. But it seemed like he just kept finding problems with me. Was I really that fat? I had never thought I was overweight. I did scroll through Instagram and Pinterest and wish that I had an hourglass figure like the models I saw, but was I really that bad looking? He also commented on my non existent boobs which I wished I could have done something about, but my fake breasts were still tucked away in my closet as far as I knew. Then there was the comment about my makeup. I had watched dozens of videos and had practiced for years, granted it wasn't every day that I could practice, but I felt like I had really improved from where I started. Then, he took me to the living room and put me on my knees to make me feel like he really did want me. But, I was left empty handed. I just can not figure Conner out.'

I was lost in my thoughts as I undressed in my bedroom and started getting ready for bed. I cleaned off my makeup before sliding into my bed and closing my eyes. A single tear ran down my cheek as I tried to tell myself everything would be ok.

The night felt long as I struggled to fall asleep. Despite how comfortable the bed was, I tossed and turned most of the night. The sun streamed across my face at dawn, but I was still tired and tried shielding myself from the light with a couple of pillows. However, it was no use. Even with the pillows over me, I couldn't possibly sleep anymore.

I sighed before throwing the blankets off of me and walking to the bathroom. As I was taking care of business, I heard a knock at my door.

"One minute!" I yelled as I finished up and made my way over to the door in my pink nightie. Opening the door, I saw the butler standing patently and waiting for me.

"Hello madam, I am to inform you that a limo will be waiting downstairs in ninety minutes. You will have a full day of appointments and you must not be late."

"Oh, ok. Where is Conner today?" I asked.

"He has already left for business, but he will be back in time for your dinner with him at 6 P.M. in the dining room."

"Ok, thank you mr..." I paused as I realized I still didn't know this man's name.

"You may call me, butler, servant, or whatever you like madam."

"Do you have a name?"

"Master prefers I do not use my name while I am on duty."

"Oh really? Would you just tell me what it is, it can be our secret."

"I am really not supposed to madam."

"I don't want to cause any trouble, I just wanted to thank you."

The butler bowed to me, "Will you be needing anything else madam?"

"No, thank you very much."

He walked down the hall as I closed the door.

I went through my new morning routine of showering, shaving, then moisturizing. I took note of Conner's comment about my makeup the previous night and was extra diligent while putting my face on. I smudged my eye liner a couple times and started over to make sure it was perfect. Once I felt my hair and makeup was adequate for Conner's standards, I walked over to the dresser and picked out a matching set of black lace panty and bra. The panties fit snugly again while the cups from the bra hung off of my chest. I sighed before walking over to the closet and looking for an outfit. Since I didn't know what I was doing today, I tried to find something that looked functional. As I looked through my choices, I quickly noticed that pants were not an option. But, I did find a black blouse and a white midi skirt that I could pair together.

I buttoned my blouse and slid my skirt on before walking over to the mirror and checking myself out. I didn't love my hair, but my makeup and outfit looked great at first glance. As I stared at my refection longer, I couldn't help but hear conner's voice creeping into my head.

'You could have done better with your makeup. Your hair looks so masculine. You'd look much better with a thinner waist and full breasts.'

I sighed before looking down over my body and feeling my chest. It did look empty, but what could I do about it. I tilted my head sideways as an idea popped into my head.

I walked over to the dresser and grabbed a few pairs of underwear. I bunched up a couple pairs before stuffing them into my bra. Shimmying my chest and pushing it around, I tried to make my torso look as naturally feminine as possible. It wasn't perfect, but I felt like it looked better than before.

Feeling like I couldn't do much more to present myself, I walked back into the closet and looked for a pair of shoes I could wear all day. I found a pair of leather knee high black high heel boots. I grabbed them from their shoe hole and sat on the bed as I zipped them on. The heels were four inches, but the shoes felt very comfortable for their shape. I walked back in front of the mirror and gave myself one more once over.

I ignored the voices in my head and smiled at my work. Despite what Conner might say, I felt beautiful. I walked over to the door and pulled the handle, but I was locked in again. I sighed loudly and stomped my foot before walking to the bed and sitting down.

I waited fifteen minutes before the butler returned and unlocked my door. I smiled at him as I exited the room even though I was slightly angry for being locked in again.

"You may follow me madam." The butler said as he began walking down the hall to the elevator. He used his key to call the elevator and waited with me for it to arrive. After a few moments, the doors opened in front of us.

We stepped in and rode the lift down to the first floor. As the doors opened, I felt a fluttering in my stomach. I was about to step out completely dressed up and take a limousine to places I wasn't even aware yet. I took a deep breath as the butler stepped out and held the elevator door open for me. I stepped onto the black and white tile floor and turned to the butler.

"When you walk out that door," he said pointing at the entrance, "There will be a black limousine waiting for you right outside. The driver has your schedule and will be driving you where you need to go today. I will see you here this afternoon."

"Do you know where I'm going?"

"I am sorry madam, all I can tell you is that your driver is waiting."

"Ok, well thank you"

"Thank you madam." He said while stepping back in the elevator and pressing a button.

I turned toward the front door and took a deep breath. I put my right foot forward and marched straight to the main entrance. Two men opened the doors for me as I approached and greeted me as I stepped out.
"Good morning Ma'am."
"How are you today miss?"
I froze up and didn't answer either of the kind gentlemen.
"Your ride is waiting for you," one of the men said as he stepped to the car and opened the door for me.
"Oh thank you very much." I said as I walked across the sidewalk to the limousine. In my heels, I needed some assistance crouching into the vehicle. I accepted the man's hand held out for me as I slid into the car. The man closed the door behind me and waved as we began driving away.

CHAPTER 5

I stared out the window as I was driven across the city. The driver stayed silent and kept his eyes on the road as we made our way to our first stop. I wanted to ask him where we were going, but I wasn't sure if either of us would get in trouble if I did. I kept my questions to myself as we pulled up to our first stop fifteen minutes into the ride.

The driver parked the car on the side of the street, and walked around to my door. He opened the door and held out his hand for me to take. I knew better than to step onto the curb in my heels without assistance and took his help. The driver nodded his head toward the salon and smiled at me. "Am I supposed to go in there?" I asked.

The driver continued smiling and pointed over to the salon. I looked at the salon then back at the driver.

"Do I have an appointment here?" I asked again.

The driver smiled and nodded while he continued pointing at the salon.

"Should I go in then?"

The driver closed the door and continued smiling while nodding at me. I started to realize that he either didn't speak English or he really didn't want to talk to me. Either way, I nodded my head to him and walked over to the double doors outside the storefront.

As I stepped inside, a lady behind the counter greeted me and asked for my name. I froze as I wasn't sure what to say. Should I give my male name or my made up female name. I hadn't shared that name with Conner or the butler, but I didn't want to give my male name to this lady I just met while crossdressed. I hesitated before answering her, "Ummm, Conner Wellington sent me?"

"Ohhhh, yes yes yes. We are ready for you. Here, come with me."

I followed the short blonde woman through the salon to a back room. Inside was a rotating chair sitting in front of a large mirror. She showed me to the seat and stood behind the chair as I sat down.

"Jessica will be right with you."
"Thank you." I answered back. She smiled before walking back out to the front area.

I began to get nervous as I sat in this private room alone. I had no idea what to expect or what was going on. While I had always fantasied about going into a salon and getting made up into a beautiful woman, but I had never actually acted on it. I twiddled my thumbs as I awaited Jessica.

She appeared a few moments later and walked behind me.
"Hey girl, how are you doing today." Jessica asked.
"Oh, I'm good." I answered timidly.
"That's good sugar, now let's see what we have to work with."
She began running her fingers through my hair and pulling it to each side. She tilted her head sideways as she meticulously studied my brown wavy hair.
"Girl, you are beautiful. I'm just going to enhance what you already have working for you. How does that sound?"
"That sounds great."
"You just relax while I start on your nails, you're in good hands."

Jessica walked over to the other side of the room and returned with a tray of various nail polish colors.
"I feel like a classic red would compliment you well. What do you think?" Jessica asked as she held up a tube of deep red nail polish.
"I do love that color." I added.
"Then its decided. Why don't you tell me a little bit about yourself?" Jessica asked as she began prepping my nails.
"Well I don't really know where to start."
"How about with your family or friends?"
"Well, my parents live in Vermont along with my three older sisters."
"Three older sisters? So you were the baby girl in the family?"
"Yeah something like that." I said curling up.
Jessica could sense I was uncomfortable with the subject and began focusing more intently on my nails. She applied the base layer to each of my nails on my left hand before letting it set under a light. She moved on to my right hand and applied a base layer to each nail again before letting them cure under the light. She began applying the red in small smooth strokes over each nail on my left hand. Once the first layer was applied, she began

working on the first layer for my right hand. She finished off each of my nails with a second layer before letting my nails dry under the light on the counter in front of me.

"What do you think?" She asked.

"Oh my god they're beautiful."

"Thank you darling. Shall we start on your toe nails in the same color?"

"Yes please." I said as I began unzipping my boots and sliding them off.

Jessica knelt down and began running through the same process on each of my toe nails.

"So are all of your friends still back in Vermont as well?" She asked.

"Yeah, all three of them." I added.

"So you really didn't leave much behind when you moved here?"

"No not really. I felt like I needed to leave since I was thirteen. I just felt like no one really understood me in that small town. It was a small town with small minded people."

"I'm sorry about that darling."

"Oh it's not your fault. I couldn't be happier now."

"Thats great darling. Now make sure to keep still while your nails dry ok?" Jessica said as she finished my last toe nail in the same matching color to my finger nails. I looked down at my nails in disbelief. Not only were they painted a classic red I had always adored, but they were done professionally. Jessica took the tray of nail polish back to the other side of the room before coming back behind me.

"Alright, now it's time for your hair." Jessica said looking at me through the mirror.

Jessica brought me over to a washing station and sat me down in front of it. She held my hair under the sink and began washing. I was overcome with the smell of flowery fragrances as she shampooed and conditioned my long flowing hair. I closed my eyes and enjoyed myself as she massaged my scalp and put me at ease.

Once my hair was washed to her liking, she brought me back to the chair and began combing it out. I loved the feelings washing over me and closed my eyes as she continued working.

"You just relax honey." She said as she began using her scissors sparingly behind my head.

I lost track of time as I fell in love with the feeling of being pampered by Jessica. She made me feel like the most special girl in the world as I sat in her care.

"So what do you have planned for the rest of the day?" She asked.

"I really don't know?" I answered.

"Ah so you're just taking the day off and enjoying yourself?"

"Yeah I guess you could say that."

"I heard that Conner sent you in, that must be fun hanging out with the big man of the city."

"Yeah he seems really special, but I don't really feel like I know him yet."

"Honey, I've been married fifteen years and I still don't feel like I know my husband. Last week, he told me he wants to become an airline pilot. Im like, 'Steve, you're afraid of flying and you get motion sickness anytime you step into the car.' But of course he thinks he knows what he's talking about and now he's reading a whole bunch of articles about how to become a pilot."

"Do you mind if I ask you a personal question?"

"Girl, my whole job is personal."

"Did you feel like you weren't pretty enough for him when you started dating?"

Jessica stopped what she was doing and looked me in the eyes.

"Of course baby. Hell, I still feel that way sometimes. But, when my man takes me by the hand and ravages me in the bedroom, all of that just disappears."

"Oh really?" I said with anxiety creeping up inside of me.

"Have you and Conner gone there yet?"

I began getting nervous and looked away before answering. "I thought we might last night but I guess he wasn't ready yet."

"I'm sure you'll get there. It's on every man's mind."

I smiled at Jessica as she finished up with my hair. We were together an hour, but I felt like I could talk to her about anything.

"Well darling, what do you think?"

I looked at myself in the mirror and was shocked at what I saw. My hair fell down just past my shoulders with slight curls at the end. It was a dark brown at the roots, but was dyed a fiery red that fell down past my face and to my upper back. I had never dyed my hair before and had to take it in for a moment. As I stared at the reflection longer, I started to fall in love with the feminine style Jessica gave me. I turned my head to each side and pushed up on my hair as I complimented her work.

"Oh my god it looks amazing!" I squealed.

"Thank you darling."

"No thank you!"

"Well you're not done yet, you get the full package today darling. Im going to go wash my hands then we can get started on your makeup."

My excitement turned to nervousness as Jessica came towards me with with a towel and wipes. I felt like my makeup provided a shield for my identity. Behind my face of makeup, I concealed my male self from the world, but Jessica was about to wipe it clean.

"Wait, do you have to do that?" I asked while putting my hand out.

"Honey, if I don't wipe it off and start clean, its simply not going to look right."

"But are you sure?"

"Just lay your head back and relax. I'm here to take care of you."

I let out a long exhale and rested my head. I closed my eyes and let Jessica clean the makeup off of my face.

As I sat with my eyes closed, I kept waiting for a gasp or the moment she realized I was a man and asked about it. But, that moment never came. She had my face clean and ready for primer within a few minutes and asked me to open my eyes as she did.

"See this honey, you're going to want to start with this before you dive into the foundation. You have to get the base right for everything else to work on top of it."

I breathed a sigh of relief before paying close attention to her methods.

She talked me through each step of the process as she applied my foundation, highlighter, three separate powders, eye liner, eye shadow, mascara, lip liner, and finally some all day lip stain. I felt like I had a much better grasp on the whole process after she explained each part in great detail. Jessica stepped behind me after she finished and admired her creation in the mirror.

"What do you think girl?"

"Wow…I mean, just wow."

I couldn't believe I was staring at my own reflection in front of me. Everything about my head exuded femininity. The contouring around my nose and cheeks gave the appearance of a small dainty nose and high defined cheek bones. I admired my eye liner that was actually perfect for once. It circled my eyes thinly and had a small wing at the side of each eye. My lips looked as full and luscious as ever, painted in a matching color to my fingernails and toenails.

As I took in the incredible job Jessica had done with my hair and makeup, Jessica began cleaning up.

"Well I hope you enjoyed yourself today, I hope to see you again soon darling."

I wasn't aware of my schedule so I smiled and agreed. "Oh yes, I hope sooner rather than later. Thank you so much Jessica."

"It was my pleasure."

I took one more look at myself in the mirror before I headed back through the salon to the front entrance. Waiting by the curb, the driver was holding the door open to the limousine while smiling politely at me.

"Oh thank you very much." I said as I stepped into the vehicle. The driver continued smiling and nodded before closing the door. He walked back over to the driver's seat and drove me to my next stop.

CHAPTER 6

Fighting traffic through the heart of the city, we arrived at an eight story office building after a twenty minute drive. The driver pulled over next to the curb and put the vehicle in park.
"Where are we now?" I asked.
The driver turned around to me and held out a card. He pointed at the name on the card, then pointed at a directory board outside the building. He handed me the card then pointed at the building again. I was starting to become frustrated with the communication barrier.
"I'm supposed to go inside and see…Doctor Bentenhousen?"
He smiled and nodded at me. I really couldn't be sure if he knew what he was nodding at.
"Should I run through a fire after?" I said keeping the same face.
The driver continued nodding and smiling.
"You don't speak any English do you?"
Once again, he continued nodding and smiling. I rolled my eyes as I watched him open his door and walk around to mine. He opened the door and held his hand out. I took his hand and stepped out before walking up to the office building.

I found Dr. Bentenhousen on the board and observed his suite was 609 on the sixth floor. I walked over to the elevator and took it to the doctor's floor. After a short walk down a narrow carpeted hallway, I arrived at my destination. As I opened the door, I was greeted by a nurse sitting behind the counter.
"Hello, Mrs. Wellington?" She asked.
I looked behind me before realizing she was referring to me. "Oh yes, I think I have an appointment?"
"Yes, come right this way."
She lead me down a short hallway and guided me to a small examination room.
"The doctor will be right with you."

"Thank you."

I looked around the room as I sat nervously waiting for the doctor. I had no idea why I was here or where I was going next. I enjoyed my time at the salon, but something about a doctor's office scared me. I shifted in my seat as I saw the knob turn and the door open.

A man in his late fifties appeared in a white coat and tan pants. His hair was mostly white, but had speckles of brown remaining. His smile was disarming as he greeted me.

"Hello Mrs. Wellington, how are you today?"

"Oh, I'm good thank you."

"Good, I have already spoken with someone from your staff and they have filled me in on what you're looking for."

"Oh, that's great." I said softly.

"I would just like to run through a few questions with you, ok?"

"Ok."

"Do you wish to live as a woman full time?"

I swallowed my saliva as I processed what he asked me. I could feel myself growing in my panties just hearing those words coming from his mouth. I nodded my head as I spoke softy, "Yes."

"Ok, have you always wanted to be a woman?"

I squirmed in my seat as I softly answered again, "Yes."

"Would you like to surgically and chemically alter your body to fit how you feel everyday?"

My heart started pounding as I contemplated what he was asking me. I had told Conner that I was willing to do whatever he asked and fully feminize myself. He mentioned that surgery was on the table, but I didn't think I would have to commit to it so soon. I felt like I had already come so far and that I really couldn't turn back now. If I told the doctor no, Conner would eventually find out and dump me. I took a deep breath before answering the doctor.

"Yes, I want to do whatever I can."

"Ok, well this seems like a straight forward case. I am prescribing you hormones that you will take everyday starting today. It is important to take the correct dosage daily. If you miss doses or take too much, it can have unpredictable effects."

I nodded as I listened to the doctor speak while writing on his clipboard.

"Once you've been on hormones for a month, we will have you back to examine you and take the next steps."

"What are the next steps."

"We'll most likely start with a breast enhancement before going for the full facial reconstructive surgery. I was told you'd be interested in facial reconstruction of the cheeks, nose, chin, lips, and neck?"

"Uh yeah, do you know how long all of this will take?"

"If you decide to go through with everything, we will have you in your new body and finished with surgical procedures within a year. However, the hormones will keep changing your body well after."

I swallowed my saliva and looked at the floor as the doctor finished up.

"I'm going to give this to the nurse, she'll forward it to your staff and let them know where to pick up the medication. If you have any questions at all, don't hesitate to ask."

I was still processing everything I just agreed to and struggled to speak to the doctor.

"Ok...Thank you."

"Have a great day Mrs. Wellington. You will be amazed at the results. I promise."

The doctor opened the door and stepped out. I sat in the examination room a few minutes before I stood up and walked out. The nurse smiled at me as I walked to the suite exit.

"Thank you Miss. I hope you have a great day."

I smiled and waved before heading back down to the limousine waiting by the curb. The driver held my door open before helping me into the vehicle. He closed the door before stepping around to his seat and driving off.

 I stared out the window as I thought about my last visit. I was both nervous and excited about what I was starting. I knew that as soon as I started on the hormones and going in for surgeries, I would never be able to look at myself as a man again. Conner would own me and my body forever. I felt myself grow again just thinking about it.

'I would never be able to afford this on my own. This is like a once in a lifetime opportunity for me. I might regret this for the rest of my life if I do, and especially if I don't.'

 The driver pulled to a stop back at our building. One of the men working up front came to the door and opened it for me. I was beginning to enjoy

being waited on. I took his hand and stepped out of the vehicle.
"Thank you." I said politely.
"It's my pleasure miss."
I walked inside and waited for the elevator. After a short ride to Conner's penthouse, I met the butler who was waiting for me.
"Good afternoon madam, you certainly do look lovey today."
I couldn't help but blush, "Thank you."
"Dinner will be in one hour. I have been instructed that you should wait in your room until master returns."
I rolled my eyes, "Is that really necessary?"
"I am sorry madam, I am merely the messenger."
I sighed before walking down the hall back to my room. The butler followed behind and stood in the doorway, "would you like anything before dinner?"
"How about some freedom?"
"I am very sorry Madam." The butler said as he closed the door and locked it.
I walked over to my window and stared out at the city.

CHAPTER 7

After a few minutes of gazing out on the city, I decided I should change into something sexier for Conner. I was still upset about the way the night ended the previous night. Maybe with a new outfit to go with my perfectly painted nails, flawless makeup, and fiery red hair, I could entice Conner into making me feel like a real woman.

I stripped down completely naked before walking to the dresser and looking for a lingerie set. I grabbed a set of red lace panties and bra along with some black fishnet stockings. I slid the panties up my hairless legs and fastened the bra behind my back. I took my time as I slid the fishnet stockings up my smooth legs as I enjoyed every moment of it.

Walking over to the closet, I stepped inside and looked for something to draw attention to myself. My eyes immediately landed on a short red dress that matched my underwear. I had to suck in my gut, but I managed to pull the dress up and get it zipped up to my mid back. I grabbed a pair of red five inch high heel pumps and slid them on as I held onto the closet door.

Stepping in front of the mirror, I checked myself out to make sure everything was perfect for Conner. My hair and makeup still looked immaculate. My dress was low cut with two small straps that came over my shoulders. The dress came down to my upper thighs and just barely covered my butt. My legs exuded sex as they were encased in fishnet stockings and the highest of red heels. I smiled from ear to ear as I admired my reflection.

I spent the next fifteen minutes in front of the mirror before the butler came to my door and announced dinner.
"Are you ready madam?" He asked.
"Yes of course." I said walking to the door eagerly.

I walked ahead of the butler down the hall and marched straight into the dining room. The room was empty as I expected, so I sat in my seat next to Conner's again. The butler walked behind me to the wall and joined me in silence as we stared out the large windows across from the table.

Like clockwork, Conner appeared a few moments later and sat in his chair at the head of the table. He was wearing a white button down shirt with a vest over top. It looked like he had ditched a blazer and tie just before walking into the room. As he sat down next to me, I looked over to him and smiled.

Conner gazed into my eyes, "You look better today."

It wasn't the compliment I was hoping for, but it was a start. "Thank you. Jessica did a really good job with…"

"I heard the doctor prescribed you some medicine, have you taken it yet?" He interrupted.

"Oh, I um, thought someone else was picking it up?" I said shyly.

"Yes madam, I have taken the liberty of preparing your dose for today." The butler said as he leaned over my shoulder and dropped two pink pills on my plate.

Conner stared at me as the butler made his way to the kitchen.

"Well, aren't you going to take it?" He asked.

I began to get nervous as I stared at the pills on my plate. I thought to myself, 'here goes nothing', as I grabbed the pills and threw them into my mouth. With one gulp of water, Conner finally broke a smile.

The butler returned a few moments later with salads in hand. Today, we were served a cucumber tomato salad with onions and mozzarella. I didn't usually eat so many vegetables, but with the balsamic dressing and seasoning, I devoured every bit of it. Our dishes were pulled away before Conner was served a Hong Kong style halibut with bok choy, sticky rice, and a ginger sauce. I didn't eat much fish, but I was drooling over Conner's dish.

As Conner saw how hungry I was and my longing for his plate, he cut off a piece of fish and scooped some rice with it before offering it to me on his fork. I smiled and leaned in for a taste. The combination of flavors melted in my mouth as I sat back in my chair. Conner smiled at me before taking another bite.

"Now that your on your medication, it won't be long before your body changes and you can eat this with me."

"I literally can't wait." I responded

Once Conner finished, the butler came and removed all of the remaining plates. Conner stood up and asked me to join him before I took his hand and followed him to the living room. It felt like we were reliving the pre-

vious night and I had another chance to impress Conner. We walked over to the glass windows overlooking the city and stood in front of them with Conner behind me.
"It just gets better every night." I observed.
"It really does." Conner agreed.
I turned around to face Conner and looked deep into his eyes. He stared back as I reached toward his middle and began feeling for his privates. As my hand wrapped around him, my gaze widened. He was at least twice my size and he didn't even feel aroused yet. I began moving my hand up and down from his base to his tip as I kept my gaze into his eyes.

    We remained in silence as I stroked him in the living room. I could feel him becoming more firm and growing in my hand as I continued. He smiled as he looked down at me.
"Are you sure you're ready for this?"
I continued stroking him as I answered, "Yes please."
Conner smiled before grabbing my arm and stopping it halfway through its motion.

    Conner lead me by the arm down the hall past his bedroom. He opened up a door at the end of the hall and lead me inside. Conner flipped on the lights to bring the room from pitch black to a dim glow. I realized immediately that this was not another bedroom. We just stepped into Conner's BDSM dungeon.

    The room was kept dark by a lack of windows and very dim lighting. As I was pulled across the room, I observed leather restraints, whips, chains, and gags hanging from the walls and laid out on a dresser against the back wall. A cage large enough for a person was on one side of the dresser with some sort of bed on the other side. Another contraption was placed in the corner next to the door we walked through, but I couldn't get a good look at what it was. Conner lead me over to the dresser next to the cage and opened it up. Inside the top drawer, I saw a collection of male and female chastity devices.
"Pull down your panties." He ordered.
I jittered as I reached up my dress and did as he instructed. Conner didn't like my fane modesty and pulled my dress up to reveal my tiny appendage hanging between my legs.
"Oh wow, we can go small right away." Conner giggled.

He reached into the drawer and pushed a few devices to the side before selecting a small male chastity cage. When hard, I measured myself growing out to be a few inches, but this cage could not have been any larger than an inch. I didn't have any previous experience with chastity, but I knew better than to ask questions.

Conner detached the ring from the base of the chastity cage before sliding the ring around my appendage. I could feel myself becoming aroused as Conner handled my junk in front of me.

"Thats like really tight." I complained.

"Thats the point. Now hold still."

Conner brought the phallic shaped cage to my middle and pressed the cage against me. My appendage was squished as it slid into the cage and just barely fit inside. Conner attached the cage to the ring around my base and used a small lock to keep it in place.

Conner let go of my member and the cage around it before letting it hang between my legs. My middle had never felt so useless as it dangled off of me. I gulped as I watched Conner reach back into the drawer and pull out a pair of steel hand cuffs.

Conner turned me around in front of him and took a hold of my wrists behind me. Even though I didn't fight back, Conner held a tight grip before fastening the steel cuffs onto me. He grabbed me by my shoulders and spun me around in front of him. Picking up a small circular ring with leather straps attached to it, he held the two straps as he forced the ring into my mouth. My mouth was propped wide open as the circular ring slid between my upper and lower teeth. I struggled to keep my balance as he pulled the straps behind my head and fastened them tightly. I moaned through the gag as I realized how far open my mouth would be stuck.

I felt completely helpless standing in front of him with my mouth open and easy to access. He put his hands on my shoulders and pushed me down to my knees. I could not have felt more submissive kneeling in front of him, unable to resist anything he put in my mouth.

Conner began teasing me by running his pinky around my lips. Salvia began to build up as I stared up at him with my mouth wide open. He moved his pinky inside my mouth and began rubbing it against my tongue. I held frozen in place as I continued staring up at him. Conner brought his index finger and thumb into my mouth and pinched my tongue before pulling it out. I left my tongue hanging out of my mouth as he began unbuttoning his pants.

My eyes fell to Conner's middle as he pulled down his pants. I started to breath heavier as I saw how large the bulge was in his underwear. My heart started pounding as he grabbed the waistband and slowly lowered it to his thighs. I was head to head with Conner while my arms were cuffed behind me and my mouth was propped wide open from a metal ring gag. I felt blood rush to my middle as I saw Conner growing in front of me.

I looked up to Conner's eyes as he stood in front of me completely exposed. He smiled as he looked back and began stroking himself. As I stared into his eyes, I could tell that he was truly proud of how large he was. There wasn't a shadow of doubt or insecurity for having just exposed himself to me. I almost felt like I should have thanked him.

I brought my eyes back in front of me as he slowly guided himself forward toward my opening. Saliva was pooling in my mouth as the anticipation grew. I closed my eyes as his tip gently pressed against my tongue. 'This is it, this is what I've been waiting for' I thought to myself.

He pushed himself forward further into my mouth as he continued pressing against my tongue. His tip passed through the ring in my mouth with no problem, but as he pushed himself all the way in, his girth was almost too much.

His skin pressed against the ring in my mouth as he thrust himself all the way to the back of my throat. I had practiced with dildos in the past, but when the real thing forced its way down my throat, my gag reflex started acting up.

Conner grabbed the back of my head firmly as my gagging contorted my neck.
"It's ok, you'll get used to it." He said as he kept pressing himself all the way in.

I felt like he was halfway to my stomach by the time his base met my lips. I whined and moaned as tears began falling down my cheek uncontrollably. I strained against my hand cuffs as Conner finally pulled himself back out. I took a deep breath as his tip rested on my tongue again.
"Are you ready?" Conner asked rhetorically. I looked up at him and shook my head yes anyway. He smiled before grabbing my head and thrusting himself inside again.

Conner began pumping rhythmically in front of me. He began shallow, but started to force himself further as he continued. His pumping in and out triggered my gag reflex again as he held my head tightly in place. Another rush of tears streamed down my face as I rocked back and forth.

After a few minutes of constant pounding against the back of my throat, it began to feel like my gagging was fading. My eyes cleared from the tears while I felt more of a tickle at the back of my throat instead of a gag. I looked up at Conner to see that his eyes were closed and his face was seriously concentrating. I brought my eyes back down in front of me and admired the patch of public hair that was neatly groomed and shaved. I closed my eyes and started to concentrate on my own enjoyment.

The stimulation from Conner sliding in and out of my mouth, paired with the fact I was wearing a tight dress, high heels, and a pair of hand cuffs, was enough to bring me to a climax. I moaned as I felt blood starting to rush to my middle again. Unfortunately, I realized that the cage trapping my member was going to be a problem.

I started to feel a pinch around my middle as my member strained against the metal cage. I moaned louder as I felt pressure building between my legs. My member kept trying to grow, but the cage would not possibly allow it. Even before I started getting aroused, it had felt very tight around my middle. But, this was a new level of tightness.

I opened my eyes back up and looked up at Conner. His facial expression had progressed from concentrating to on the cusp of euphoria. The thought of him exploding in my mouth sent another tingle to my middle which made me feel another strain. I started whining more than moaning as Conner began thrusting faster inside of me.

I squealed as I felt the taste of precum leek onto my tongue. Every motion and sensation was causing me a mix of pleasure and pain as I was used by Conner. I looked up at his face as his body started to slow down its thrusts. His mouth opened ever so slightly as he let out a loud groan. The floodgates broke and a rush of hot salty liquid began pumping into my mouth.

I gargled and groaned as pulse after pulse was sent into my mouth. Conner held my head firmly as he slowly continued rocking in and out of me. His rock hard member pulsed repeatedly as squirt after squirt shot to the back of my throat. With my mouth propped wide open, I had a very difficult time swallowing anything. Despite my inability to clear my mouth, some still rushed straight back and down my throat.

Conner let out a huge sigh of relief as he let go of my head. I fell forward and watched as a mix of saliva, but mostly cum, oozed from my mouth. A string of liquid dropped to the floor while remaining connected to my mouth. I panted as I tried to catch my breath.
"Well, that wasn't too bad." Conner said.
I struggled to swallow the excess liquid in my mouth as I looked up to him.
"What did you think, the largest you've ever seen right?"
I shook my head yes without hesitation. Conner smiled back at me.
"You kind of look like shit. You should go wash off, but don't you dare take that cage off. I'll lock you in the other cage for a week if you try anything." He said while pointing at the cage in the corner. "I don't want to have to punish you, but I will."
I submissively nodded my head in agreement. What other option did I have anyway.

CHAPTER 8

I stood under the shower with hot water rushing over me. After Conner had released my handcuffs and gag, he retired to his bedroom as I did the same. With how worked up I had become, I was somewhat disappointed the night ended so soon. Although I was still locked up in a chastity cage, I felt like with enough stimulation I could manage to climax anyway. I held the cage in my hands as I stood in the shower thinking about my night with Conner.

'Oh my god, I can't believe he has so many toys in his dungeon. When he said feminization, I had no idea he meant all of that, and a chastity cage? I wonder how long he's planning on leaving this on me? And would if it like rusts shut or something. Does he even care if I can never get it off, or is that what he's hoping for?'

I pulled the cage from right to left as I examined the thing keeping my member from growing even the slightest bit. Now that my arousal had worn off, the cage didn't feel as tight, but I was still very aware of its presence. I wasn't a compulsive master-bater, but I felt like I needed some sort of release every few days. I was saving myself for Conner since I had arrived, but now I was starting to question if that was a good idea.

As I thought about Conner, a flash of his naked body flooded my brain. Standing in the shower, I suddenly felt like I was back in the other room on my knees with my hands tied behind me. My heart started racing as blood rushed to my middle again. I moaned in the shower as I felt the tightness return to my cage.

"Fuck, this is way too tight. I have to think about something else." I said to myself.

I tried my best to ignore my predicament and replace my thoughts with nonsexual images. After washing the conditioner from my hair, I stepped out of the shower and dried myself off. Wrapping myself in a plush white towel, I tip toed over to my bed.

Sliding between the sheets, I rested my head and shut my eyes. I struggled to fall asleep, but the excitement from my night with Conner was still wearing off. I continued playing the night in my head as I laid in the dark bedroom. I would grab my middle as pressure built behind the cage and try to steer my thoughts a different direction when it became too painful.

'He must have thought I looked pretty tonight. I mean, he wouldn't have taken me in there and done what he did to me if he didn't think so, right?'

As I played the night in my head again, I remembered looking up at him and seeing his eyes closed as he was working up to his finish.

'Why wasn't he looking at me then? What was he thinking about while I was sucking on his middle? Am I not pretty enough for him to look at? I had myself made up by a professional, I wore the most expensive clothes, and my hair was the most beautiful it had ever been, but was it still not good enough for him? Would if I go through the hormone treatment, I go through with the breast enhancement, and have every other surgery that the doctor discussed, and I'm still not pretty enough for Conner. Would if I change everything about my body so that I'm not even recognizable as a man and I never have the ability to live my male life again, and Conner gets bored with me. Would I still be happy with my decision?'

I tossed and turned in bed as I processed my feelings of doubt and self consciousness.

'Why would a rich, sexy man in his thirties still be single? Am I just the latest toy that he is playing with until he gets bored?'

I lost track of time as I laid in the bed, tossing and turning sporadically. Despite my eyes staying closed in the darkness, I couldn't have felt further from falling asleep. I had so many questions for Conner but had no idea when or how I could possibly ask him.

CHAPTER 9

Awaking the next morning, feelings of grogginess and fatigue consumed me. Between the avalanche of thoughts and questions that raced through my head, as well as the occasional pinching feeling coming from my middle, I could not have slept more than an hour. The butler knocked on my door while the sun shined through my windows. I sighed before hoping out of bed and tossing a robe around myself.

I cracked the door as I stood behind it.
"Good morning madam."
"Good morning." I responded.
"I would like to inform you that you do not have any appointments today. Conner said you should relax and rest before tonight."
"What's tonight?"
"I am merely the messenger madam."
I rolled my eyes as I sighed, "Thank you."
"Will you be needing anything this morning?"
"An omelette, bacon, and hash browns?"
"I will bring you your breakfast shortly madam."
"Thank you." I said as I pushed the door shut.

I walked over to the bathroom and turned on the faucet. I splashed some water on my face as I rubbed my eyes. After taking care of my morning business, I heard a knock at my door again. I walked back over to the door and answered it.

The butler was standing in the doorway with a shake in one hand and two pink pills in the other.
"Your breakfast madam."
"This is it?"
"Yes madam."
"Why would I expect anything else." I said as I grabbed the pills and the shake from the butler. He watched as I threw the pills in my mouth and gulped them down with the smoothie. Even though I didn't have smoothies

very often, it was surprisingly enjoyable. The butler nodded his head as I closed the door again. Hearing a click from the door, I realized he locked me in again from the other side. I rolled my eyes before taking another drink from my smoothie.

I walked over to the floor to ceiling windows and stared over the city while I enjoyed my breakfast. As I watched the busyness of the city twenty five stories below me, I couldn't help but wonder what Conner was up to. All I had known about him was that he was a wealthy man that sent a lot of emails. But beyond that, I was clueless.

After finishing my drink, I stepped back into the bathroom and began working on my makeup. After having watched Jessica apply my makeup to perfection, I was eager to use some of her techniques to replicate the look. I spent the next few hours working on my makeup and doing my best to match Jessica's artistry. Foundation felt like the easy part, but getting the mix of powders just right to contour my nose, cheeks, and chin provided to be much more challenging.

With some practice, I began to improve in some areas while I still struggled in others. I must've done and redone my eye liner over thirty times as I stood in front of the mirror. I would try to start with a thin line around my eye lids, but always ended up making it far too thick by the end. Eventually, I found my perfect medium.

After finally finishing with my makeup for the day, I walked over to the closet and began trying on some dresses. As I slid on a long pink ball gown, I could feel pressure building between my legs. I absolutely loved dressing up and the feelings it brought, but I was having a hard time enjoying myself with my member locked up and completely prevented from becoming erect. I adjusted my cage often as I walked around and twirled in front of the mirror.

Even though I had only been dieting a couple of days, I had already started to feel a difference in the waistline of my dress. The dresses still felt tight around my waist and extremely loose around my chest, but they were slightly easier to slid on now. Apparently not eating much for two days can make you drop a couple pounds quickly.

Looking through my vast selection of high heels, I enjoyed myself as I tried on various pumps, strappy sandals, high heels boots, wedges, as well as some more exotic pairs of high heels. I practiced swaying my hips and walking a straight line as I strutted around the room. Stopping in front of the full length mirror on the closet door, I would strike a pose and pucker my lips before walking to the closet and returning in another outfit.

Although I was locked in my room, I felt a freedom I hadn't felt before. I had all of the outfits, high heels, and makeup I could ever ask for, and I was encouraged to practice acting femininely. For years I had fantasized about life as a sissy, but now it was my life.

After hours of dressing up and enjoying myself, the afternoon sun turned to an orange glow over the city. With dinner fast approaching, I began contemplating which dress and high heels I should wear for Conner. I looked over my options and thought carefully.

'When I tried to go classier, I felt like Conner ignored me, but when I pulled out a sexier dress he couldn't help but have his way with me.'

My eyes locked onto a short pink dress hanging in front of me. The dress barely covered my butt and hugged my upper thighs. The top of the dress scooped low across the chest while two straps ran over my shoulders. I paired the dress with strappy pink sandals that stood with five inch heels. Sitting on my bed, I slipped the heels on and fastened the straps.

I walked in front of the mirror and puckered my lips as I checked myself out one last time. My breasts still needed more filling out, but I felt like I looked hot. As I awaited the butler to alert me for dinner. I walked over to the windows and stared out over the city

Once six o'clock rolled around, I heard a knock on my door. I walked over and answered it promptly.

"Hello madam, you look lovely this evening."

"Thank you" I said with a smile.

"Are you ready for..."

"Dinner...Yes please." I said as I stepped out in front of the butler and began walking down the hall ahead of him. I walked into the dining room and took my seat next to Conner's. We awaited his arrival as usual.

A few minutes later, Conner appeared wearing a black suit. He was wearing a white shirt with a few buttons undone underneath his black jacket. Conner sat at his seat at the head of the table before giving the signal to the butler.

"How was your day?" I asked.

Conner turned his attention toward me as he answered, "busy as ever."

"A lot of meetings?"

"Yeah, but mostly a bunch of bullshit I don't really want to talk about."

"Oh that's ok, I was just curious about what you do."

"I'm more interested in what you did today?"

"Oh, well, I had a smoothie this morning which was actually kind of delicious. Then I washed my face, shaved, and spent a few hours practicing my make up, then…" the butler walked in and served a plate as I continued, "I tried on a bunch of outfits and a bunch of high heels. I practiced walking in them, some of them are like really high and I had a difficult time at first, but I managed to get better…"

"Wow, it sounds like a full day." Conner said cutting me off.

"Well, yeah it kinda was. I could use some more practice with my makeup but I felt like I did an ok job at the end."

"It looks fine tonight."

"Oh, thank you." I said looking down at my salad in front of me. I was so busy talking that I didn't realize the butler already served it.

"You didn't have any trouble with the cage did you?"

"That? Well, it felt kind of tight and pinched a few times."

"But you didn't take it off did you?"

"Well, no of course not. I don't think I could if I tried."

"Good."

"Why do you want me wearing it?" I asked.

"Conner paused before answering, "Because you need to learn to enjoy yourself without using that. If you are going to fully feminize yourself for me, that means giving up everything male."

"You mean…"

"Yes…constant use of the cage with the hormones will shrink it and teach you to enjoy yourself without even touching there. Once you can manage without it…" Conner stared at me as he took the last bite of his salad.

I swallowed my saliva as I took in what Conner was explaining. If I stayed with him, I would never touch my middle again. I nibbled on my salad as I sat and thought to myself.

    The butler returned a few minutes later with a steak for Conner. I was left with only a salad again. However, with my restricted diet, I was starting to feel full from the small salad anyway. I watched as Conner devoured his food before wiping his mouth with a white napkin. He stood from his chair and held out his hand. I took his hand and followed him out of the dining room.

We skipped the living room and headed straight down the hall to Conner's special room. He let go of my hand as we entered the room and shut the door behind us. I stood and waited for whatever Conner desired next.

CHAPTER 10

Conner circled me like a predator does its prey. I stared straight ahead at the wall as he studied my body from head to painted toes. He walked to a metal contraption in the corner of the room before calling me over using his finger. I put my head down and walked to him submissively.

Conner took my hand and helped me onto the contraption. As I stepped up, my waist pressed against a bar while my arms rested on two pads in front of me. My knees and ankles rested on another set of pads while my feet dangled off the ends. The device made it so that I was bent over a large center bar while on my forearms and knees. Conner walked in front of me and began fastening the wrist cuffs attached to the pads.

After tightening my wrists restraints, he walked behind me and did the same with my ankles. With the bar running underneath my waist and my wrists and ankles tied down, I was allowed very little movement. The most I could manage from my lower half was to sway my butt from side to side. On my upper half, I could move my neck and head around, but Conner was about to change that.

Conner grabbed a large ball gag from the dresser before sliding it into my mouth. Moans escaped me as he pulled the gag tightly behind my head and fastened it. He walked to the dresser and returned with a leather neck corset. As he slid it around my neck, I could feel the neck corset start at my collarbones and run up to just below my nose. Once Conner had the neck corset positioned correctly, he began lacing it firmly.

I felt the leather compressing tightly against the ball gag in my mouth and encasing my neck. As he finished tightening the lacing behind me, I was completely unable to move my neck. I moaned as I struggled against the leather material keeping my head facing straight down in front of me. I looked to my right with only my eyes to see what Conner was grabbing for me next. I struggled to make out a long object and bottle in Conner's hand as he walked behind me.

I screamed as Conner slapped my ass as hard as he could. With my mouth completely covered, my high pitch squeal came out as a soft whimper. He slapped both of his hands on my rear and began rubbing it. I cooed as I felt his large muscular hands caressing my soft behind. I began purring as he pulled up my short dress and revealed my panties.

I closed my eyes and melted as he continued rubbing my rear. His hands against my soft skin and lace panties was starting to arouse me. I moaned as I felt my trapped middle strain against its cage. I whimpered through my gag and neck corset while I felt Conner pull down my panties and keep massaging me.

As the arousal continued to build in my cage, I began breathing heavier through my nose. Although I was enjoying myself, the stimulation Conner was giving me had become more painful than pleasurable. My caged middle ached to be released and wanted nothing more than a small orgasm. I moaned as I thought to myself, 'I wish he would just let me go already. I would literally do anything for a release right now.'

Conner granted my wish, although not in the way I was expecting. I felt a large object begin pressing between my cheeks as Conner held one hand on my left cheek. The slimy object pushed its way up to my opening before it met some resistance. I moaned as loud as I could through my gag and tried shaking my butt back and forth. With how Conner restrained me, there was no way to fight what was about to happen.

The slimy rod continued pressing harder against my hole until I couldn't fight it anymore. I gulped as it entered behind me. My cheeks felt like they were going to split in two as this object slid its way further and further inside. I began screaming into the gag, but the only thing that came out were muffled whines. There was nothing I could do but accept what Conner was doing.

I could feel the object continue moving in until Conner's right hand met my cheeks. He stopped before pulling it all the back out of me. My rear regained its shape for a moment before the object pressed back inside. I whimpered as I felt it begin to slide in and out repeatedly. Conner slapped my behind as he made me feel like a real woman.

Conner's left hand began massaging my cheeks as his right hand moved the large dildo in and out rhythmically. I breathed heavily as the sensations started to become more pleasurable. I began to feel blood rushing to my middle as the stimulation in my rear intensified.

I groaned as loud as I could as I felt the cage keeping me from growing. Despite my inability to become erect, I could still feel an orgasm building inside of me. I swallowed the saliva in my mouth and tried to control my breathing as Conner speed up his motion. The dildo was pumping in and out faster and faster as I started letting out high pitch whimpers. Conner had found a special spot that was putting me right over the edge.

The sensations and feelings coming from my behind were all new to me as Conner continued. Without any stimulation to my trapped member, I still felt like a climax about to overtake me. I tensed up my behind as I felt the pressure making its way up. I was about to explode any second while still completely soft in my cage. It felt like my middle had given up on trying to grow as I felt the end approaching.

While Conner pumped the dildo into me as hard as he could, I could feel small squirts of liquid making its way out with each thrust from Conner. He was completely in control as he pumped out squirt after squirt from my middle. I moaned in pleasure as I felt the strongest climax I had ever experienced.

Shivers started from my butt and worked their way up my spine. I could hardly control my breathing as the sensations worked their way through my whole body and caused me to shake uncontrollably. After a few moments, I began calming down and regaining some self control.

Conner continued pumping the dildo in and out until I had stopped shaking from the intense experience. He gave one last thrust and left the dildo inside of me momentarily. Walking over to the dresser, he grabbed another object before returning behind me and pulling the dildo out. I whimpered as I didn't want the experience to end. I was still in ecstasy from what Conner had done and was hoping for another round. I felt like Conner could read my mind as he granted my wish for a second time. But again, it wasn't granted in quite the way I was hoping.

A soft moan escaped me as I felt another slightly larger object enter me. The object flared out wide before becoming thinner again at the base. With my behind stretched out, Conner slid the object inside of me with relative ease. Conner pushed it in until a flange pressed against my tailbone and wouldn't allow it to move any further. He pulled my panties up before pulling my dress down again.

Conner walked around in front of me and knelt down to my face. He tilted his head as he looked me in the eyes.
"This stays in at all times. Unless you are using the toilet, it will always stay in. Is that clear?"
In my neck corset, I struggled to make any noises let along nod my head. I moaned through the gag, "MHM".
Conner smiled and rose back to his feet.

I felt him undoing the lacing on my neck as I waited to be released. In a few moments, he removed the neck corset and placed it back in the drawer. My head hung down as it was finally free. Conner released the gag from behind my head and dropped it to the ground.

As my head dangled in front of Conner, he unbuttoned his pants and pulled them down to his thighs. He pulled down his underwear before grabbing the back of my head by the hair. After pulling my head upright, I was head to head with Conner for the second night in a row.

I swallowed the excess saliva in my mouth as he plunged himself forward. I moaned as he spared no time pushing himself all the way to the back of my throat. My neck strained as I began gagging on Conner's rod. As he pumped himself in and out of my mouth a few times very deeply, my gag reflex subsided.

I struggled to look up at Conner with my eyes as he held my head and thrust back and forth. His eyes were closed again as he concentrated. I moaned as loud as I could manage to try and get his attention, but his eyes stayed closed tightly. He began letting out a small moan as I felt him nearing an orgasm in my mouth. My tongue rubbed underneath his base as I felt him begin twitching and tensing up. With some help from my tongue, he was pushed right over the edge.

My mouth was flooded with hot salty liquid as Conner slowly continued rocking back and forth. I did my best to swallow what Conner squirted into me, but his load was simply too big. My mouth began overflowing and dripping as Conner released everything he had into me.

After a few moments, Conner let go of my hair and pulled out. Breathing heavily, he released me from the device that I was on and helped me off. I kept my eyes to the ground as he wished me a goodnight.
"Goodnight" Conner said as he walked out toward his bedroom.
"Goodnight master." I responded.

CHAPTER 11

Another night passed with very little sleep as I spent the night tossing and turning in my bed. Just as I started to get used to the cage trapping my member, I was given a whole new problem. With each shift of my body or movement of my behind, I would feel the pressure from the plug that had been inserted into me.

After a few hours of feeling constant pressure from the object in my rear, I managed to ignore the feeling and dose off to sleep. Awaking a couple hours later, I had almost forgotten that I was plugged. I pulled the covers over my head as I tried to shield myself from the sunlight beaming in.

After a few minutes of laying in bed, I felt a familiar morning feeling of needing to relieve myself. I rushed over to the bathroom and pulled down my lace panties that I was still wearing from the previous night. As I sat on the toilet, I reached beneath me and tried pulling out the butt plug.

Sliding out ever so slowly, I could feel the flared shape stretching me as it neared the opening. As I pulled harder, I could feel my hole stretching again to allow the plug to be removed. Once the widest part of the plug was clear, the rest followed easily. I almost couldn't believe that the plug fit inside of me as I held it in my hand.

Once I took care of my business, I cleaned myself and the plug thoroughly before trying to reinsert it. While struggling to push it back inside, I could feel that my muscles had tightened back up again. Looking around the bathroom, I found a few bottles of lube underneath the sink. I lathered the plug with plenty of lube before attempting to push it in again.

I bent over with one hand on the sink while the other pushed the plug between my cheeks. As I took a deep breath and relaxed, I could feel the plug slide right back into place. It felt like it returned home as my behind accepted the object.

I went through the rest of my morning routine by showering and shaving before washing my face and doing my makeup. From all of the practice the previous day, I managed to perfect my makeup a little quicker. Once my face was put on, I was ready to get dressed. I slid into a matching pair of white lace panties and bra before making my way to the closet. Inside, I found a beautiful white form fitting dress. It was knee length with a round neck at the top and lace long sleeves. After having been ravaged the previous night, it felt nice to wear something more modest.

I slid into a pair of white high heel pumps before walking over to the mirror and checking myself. I puckered my bright red lips and blew myself a kiss as I stood in front of the mirror. With my full face of makeup, beautiful dress, and high heels, I looked as feminine as I felt on the inside. I had become more comfortable looking at my feminine self than my male alter ego.

I walked over to the bed and sat as I waited for the butler to come for me. After a short wait, I heard a knock at the door. The butler entered my room as I stood up from the bed.

"Good morning." I greeted.

"Good morning madam. I have your breakfast for you. He held out a smoothie and the two pink pills. I took them from his hands and swallowed the pills with a gulp from the smoothie.

"So am I staying here again today?"

"Yes madam. Conner will be away on business for a couple weeks and would like if you remained here while he is away."

"Why didn't he mention it last night?"

"I'm sorry madam, it was a spur of the moment trip. He said that he will return as soon as possible."

"Do I have to stay locked in here the whole time he's away?"

"I'm afraid so madam. However, he did say that if you 'behave' while he is away, he will reconsider this policy when he returns."

"Well, thank you?"

"It's my pleasure madam." The butler said as he closed the door and locked it again.

I sighed before walking over to the window.

'He went away for two whole weeks and didn't even say anything? What am I supposed to do while he's gone? I mean, I could practice my make up some more, and I do need to get better at working on my hair.'

After gazing out on the city and losing myself in my thoughts for a while, I headed to the bathroom and tried to be constructive with my time.

I spent the rest of my day in front of the mirror practicing my makeup application incessantly. Without a dinner to attend with Conner, I had no deadline for when I needed to be ready and dressed. I utilized the time to practice my technique until the butler brought me a salad for dinner. I took a short break while eating, but returned to my makeup immediately after.

I arose the next morning to the butler and another dose of my breakfast with pills. After gulping down the pills in front of the butler, I returned to my mirror again. I was determined to practice until perfection while Conner was away.

Another day came and passed with my same routine. I had forgotten about my cage as my plug was the only thing I could find myself thinking about. Each movement and shift of my body came with a renewed feeling that something was stuck up inside of me. I tried my best to focus on my makeup and forget, but it was no use.

A few more days passed before the butler updated me on Conner's return plans.
"Yes, he seemed to have a bit of trouble and may be gone a little longer now. I will let you know as soon as I know more." The butler informed.
"Is he ok? Do you know what happened?" I asked feeling concerned.
"I'm sorry madam, I do not have anything more for you right now, but I will keep you informed as I am."
I thanked the butler before he left me alone in my room again.

After having spent a week on my strict diet, I started to notice the results taking effect. My waist felt thinner as I was able to slide into my dresses easier. They were still a little tight at the waist and loose in the chest, but the tightness was no where near where it was when I first arrived. I couldn't be certain, but I also felt like the hormones were shifting some of my weight to my chest.

I had never had much meat on my chest, but I couldn't help noticing my body starting to change. With the little extra fat that formed, I felt like I had achieved a small A cup. This was still nothing compared to the bras and dresses in my closet that were fitted for an E cup, but it was a pleasant start. I found myself unable to keep myself from rubbing my nipples as they became more sensitive.

Another week passed with no news from the butler. I started to notice that aside from the development happening with my chest, my arms and legs were having a reverse effect. I was never a body builder, but with my strict dieting and hormone treatment, it felt like my arms were thinning out significantly. Seeing how thin my arms looked, I attempted flexing in front of the mirror. A slight bump raised on my bicep but it remained mostly flat. I brought them down and tried flexing again, but there clearly was not much muscle present.

After another week on my strict diet of hormones, smoothies, and salads, I was at my thinnest I had been since high school. Although I was losing weight on my stomach, arms, and legs, my A cup breasts remained on my chest. One month of hormones started to show its results with small round breasts starting to bud. With my waist down a few inches, the roundness of my chest started to present itself.

After four weeks of staying locked in my room, the butler informed me of an appointment I had.
"Where is my appointment?" I asked.
"You have an appointment with Dr. Bentenhousen."
"Do you have any news on Conner? Its felt like forever since I've seen him."
"I'm afraid he is going to be a few more days madam. Your appointment is this morning so you will need to be ready within an hour."
"Fine, I'll be ready soon."
"Thank you madam."

I rushed through my morning routine as I scrambled to get ready. Having spent weeks working on my makeup application, I had become proficient in my technique. In less than thirty minutes I applied a basic look with foundation, setting powder, blush, eye shadow, eye liner, mascara, lip liner and lipstick. Once my face was on, I slid into a pair of tan panties and bra before going to the closet and picking out a pink pencil skirt and a white blouse. I finished up my outfit with a pair of tan stiletto pumps.

It wasn't long before the butler returned and informed me that the driver was waiting. I followed the butler down to the main entrance before meeting the driver at the curb outside of the building. He smiled and nodded as he opened the limousine door for me. I smiled as I sat inside and waited to be taken to my destination.

We arrived at the doctor's office where the driver stepped out of the vehicle and ran around to my door to open it. I stepped outside with his help and nodded before heading to the building. I took the elevator up to the doctor's floor and proceeded to his suite number 609.

A nurse greeted me before I was escorted to the back room.
"The doctor will be with you momentarily."
I nodded my head as I sat nervously.
Dr. Bentenhousen knocked on the door before coming in a few moments later.
"Hello, how are you doing today?"
"Oh, good thank you." I responded.
"Good, I see today we have you scheduled for your first breast augmentation."
"My first one?" I asked.
"Yes, we had it set up to put you in a C cup today, then jump to an E cup a couple months from now. Some girls like to augment themselves in steps so that they can adjust to their new bodies over time."
"But I would have two surgeries and get E cups anyway?"
"Yes, but we'll put you out and I promise you won't feel a thing."
"Could we just skip the second surgery and go straight to an E today?" I asked.
"We could, but that big of a change can be a lot for someone."
"I can handle it."
"It's not too late to adjust the size, but are you sure you want to do this?"
"Yes, I would just prefer as few surgeries as possible."
"As you wish Mrs. Wellington. Just stay here while I go make the changes."

CHAPTER 12

After awaking from the general anesthetics, I felt groggy and light-headed. The nurse helped me to the car while the driver opened the door for me. I sat inside the limousine and closed my eyes as the driver proceeded to take me home. I couldn't remember where I was or where I was going until halfway through the ride.

With each bump of the road and movement in my seat, a completely new feeling engulfed me. I looked down to the two melons attached to my chest and watched as they jiggled underneath the bandages. Even with the tight wrapping holding them in place, I could still feel every irregularity of the road we were traveling on. I crossed my arms and held my breasts tight through the ride home.

After a restless trip across the city, I arrived back home. I was helped out of the car and let into the building by the workers before heading to the elevator. After a short ride up to the penthouse, the butler stood in the entranceway waiting for me.

"Hello madam. How are you feeling?" He asked.

"I'm feeling kind of dizzy right now." I answered.

"Here, let me help you to your room so you can lay down."

The butler took my arm and guided me to my bed. He helped me slide under the covers before turning off the lights and closing the door. I dozed off to sleep within a few seconds of my head hitting the pillows.

I slept like a rock until the next morning when the butler prodded my shoulder.

"What? What's going on?" I said while rubbing my eyes.

"I was just checking that you're alright. You've been out for 15 hours madam." The butler stated.

"What?" I said as I slowly sat up in bed.

I could feel the full weight of my breasts as they shifted and began pulling on the bandages. Putting my arms under my cleavage, I held up some of the excess weight. After blinking my eyes a few times, I turned toward the butler standing next to the bed.

"Do you know where Conner is yet?" I asked.

"Yes madam, he will be returning next week."

"He will?" I said lighting up.

"Yes madam, now relax and I will return with your breakfast."

"Ok thank you."

Throwing the covers off of me, I slid my feet down to the floor and stood up from the bed. As I arose to my feet, I could feel my chest bounce and jiggle with every movement to the bathroom. Having had a flat chest my entire life, my center of gravity had to readjust to the new weight distribution in my body. I brought my arms under my chest and held some of the weight as I tip toed across the room.

As I walked into the bathroom, I caught the first look at myself since the surgery. I was stunned as I looked at the figure in the mirror. Having spent a month on strict dieting and hormones, paired with a set of some of the largest breasts I'd ever seen, I felt like I was dreaming as I checked myself out. My waist was the thinnest I had ever been, my arms had lost all resemblance of belonging to a man, and my chest was absolutely massive. Even with the tight bandaging keeping my breasts pressed up against my body, there was no hiding how large they had become.

I spent twenty minutes standing in front of the mirror in awe of my body. After having spent years fantasizing about what it would be like to have a set of boobs of my own, I was having trouble processing the fact that these E cup breasts were actually mine. I turned from side to side, pushing up on each cup while I examined myself. Feeling slight irritation from having just went through surgery, I was very careful caressing myself.

As I stood in the bathroom, a familiar morning feeling was creeping up. I pulled down my panties and sat on the toilet. I wiped my cage clean after reliving myself but felt there was more. Remembering that I was still plugged, I stood up and leaned over the sink. I reached behind me and grabbed a hold of the plug that was sitting snuggly in place. As I gave a tug to pull it out, I could feel that it had settled into place after being left for over 20 hours.

I let out a whimper as I felt myself stretching to let the widest part of the plug pass. Feeling pressure as I pulled, I began shaking up and down as I gave small tugs to the plug. With each shake and bounce of my body, I could feel my breasts bouncing tenfold. The sensitivity caused me to moan louder as the plug neared its exit.

Finally removing the plug, I sat on the toilet and finished my business in the bathroom. After cleaning and reinserting the plug, I walked back out to my bedroom and slid into bed. Although I had slept most of the previous day away, I was still feeling groggy and tired. I heard the butler knock on my door as I sat on my bed.

"Yes?" I called out.

"I have your breakfast madam." The butler answered as he stepped into my room.

The butler handed me my smoothie and pills as I sat on my bed. He watched as I gulped everything down before laying back in bed.

"I will leave you to rest madam."

"Thank you." I said as I laid my head down.

After another day of rest and relaxation in my room, the grogginess faded along with my fatigue. By the next day, I was starting to feel like myself again. The nurse had given instructions to rest and keep my bandages around my breasts at all times for the next week, unless I was showering. I followed her instructions and took it easy while I recovered.

As I spent the next week waiting for Conner to return and for my breasts to recover, I felt like a child waiting to unwrap my presents on Christmas. I could not resist trying on a few outfits in my new body, but mostly stayed in a robe through the course of the week. As the days dragged on, I spent most of my time staring out the window, imagining what Conner would say when he returned and saw me.

As the week drew to a close, it was my last night wearing my itchy bandages. I could not wait to be finished and back in my bras again. The butler returned to my room after I finished my salad for dinner.

"Are you finished?" He asked.

"Yes thank you." I said.

"Will there be anything else?"

"Do you know when Conner will be home yet?" I asked.

"I just heard that he will be returning tomorrow evening madam."

"Do you know what time?"

"It will be just after dinner madam."

"Ok thank you."
"It is my pleasure madam."
After the butler left my room, I laid on my pillow while feeling restless for what tomorrow would bring.

CHAPTER 13

Finally, today was the day. Conner was arriving this evening and these uncomfortable bandages could be removed for good. I arose from my bed and scampered over to the bathroom. After carefully unwrapping the bandages, my breasts could breath freely. As the last bit of wrap slid off of my chest and they were completely exposed, I could feel the weight of each hanging off of me.

After feeling the boob sweat underneath my cleavage, I stepped into the shower and began my morning routine of showering and shaving. Once I was finished in the shower, I decided to spend some extra time on my makeup this morning. With Conner coming back tonight, I wanted to do my best to impress him. I applied my foundation evenly and made sure that it dried before using some powders to contour my nose, cheeks, and chin. I drew on my eyebrows with a thin line from my eye brow pencil before moving on to my eye makeup. Starting with my eyeliner, I encircled my eyes and gave a small wing at the end of each. I applied some dark eye shadow before using extra volume mascara for my lashes. Before applying my lip makeup, I walked to the dresser and searched for underwear.

After picking out a pink lacy pair of panties and sliding them on, I stepped into the closet and began searching for something sexy. After a few seconds, my eyes landed on a short neon pink dress. I unzipped it from the back and stepped in before pulling it up. The dress was a perfect fit as I pulled it up over my breasts and slid my arms though the spaghetti straps. Without a bra on, my nipples popped through the fabric and left little to the imagination.

I zipped the dress up my back before picking out a matching pair of neon pink strappy stiletto high heel sandals. I latched them on and walked over to the mirror for my lipstick. I circled my lips with a neon pink lip liner before applying a matching neon pink lip stain to compliment my dress. As I stood in front of the mirror, I couldn't believe it was my reflection staring back at me.

My figure looked unrecognizable to the person I was when I first arrived. My legs looked thinner while incredibly soft and supple. My arms were much more slender and feminine. My waist had shrunk at least a few inches which accentuated my chest further. My large round breasts were perfectly shaped and extra perky in my tight dress. Aside from the appendage locked between my legs, I was a woman from head to painted toes.

I giggled to myself as I turned and twirled in front of the mirror. Conner wouldn't be returning until later in the day, but with the anxiety and anticipation that had built for over a month, I was determined to be ready for him whenever he might return.

The butler knocked on my door and let himself in as I stood in front of the mirror.
"You look lovely today." The butler stated.
"Why thank you. I can't wait to see Conner."
"I'm sure madam. Here is your breakfast." He said while holding out my smoothie and pills.
I gulped down my breakfast before returning my attention to the mirror. The butler snuck out with the empty glass and closed the door behind him as I continued checking to make sure everything was perfect.

After a couple hours of standing in front of the mirror and touching up any imperfection I could find in my makeup, I walked over to the windows and stared out on the city. I could only imagine where Conner was coming from as I had been kept in the dark regarding his absence. As I looked over the city, my mind began to wander.
'Where could Conner have gone for over a month. China? Germany? Australia? Maybe all three? What kind of business requires you to leave for so long? I just hope that I am pretty enough for him when he comes back. I mean, I've gotten way better at my makeup. My clothes actually fit perfectly now, and I jumped cup sizes so that I have these massive breasts now. He was probably just expecting to see my tiny C cups when he returned. He is going to be so happy when he sees how full and round they are as an E cup.'
I laid in my bed and rested as I began daydreaming. I imagined Conner bursting through my door upon his return and ravaging me as I laid face down on the bed. I imagined him slapping my behind while I squealed and moaned underneath him. I could almost feel him penetrating me as I laid in

bed alone with my thoughts.

As the afternoon turned to evening, the butler came to my room with my nightly dinner salad. I was so nervous about Conner's return that I could barely even finish the small plate. I ate as much as I could before leaving it for the butler to take. After my short dinner, I went back to the mirror and touched up my lip makeup. Twenty minutes later, I was sitting back on my bed counting the minutes until Conner's return.

An hour passed without a knock from the butler or Conner. I sat as patiently as I could manage while I continued to wait. When another hour passed with no sign of Conner, I laid my head on my pillow but was careful not to smudge my makeup. As another hour passed, I began to get worried. 'Where could Conner be? I thought he was coming after dinner?'
As the night went on, my eyes began to feel heavy. I rested my eyes as I laid on my bed. My eyes fluttered open every few minutes to keep myself from falling asleep, but eventually they stayed closed.

I awoke a few hours later to a hand on my shoulder. Conner had arrived.
"Are you still awake?" He asked.
"I am now." I said smiling back at him.
"Good, because its been a long day and I need something."
"Oh, what did you have in mind?" I said sitting up next to Conner.
He looked down at my breasts as he smiled. "I have a couple ideas."

I felt like Conner was practically dragging me down the hall as my breasts bounced with each step. He marched us straight to his special room as he held my arm. Shutting the door behind us, Conner walked me over to the dresser before he pulled out a pair of handcuffs and ball gag. Facing me toward the dresser, he pushed me against it roughly while he fastened the handcuffs behind my back. Grabbing the ball gag from the dresser, he brought it around my head and pulled it into my mouth. I opened my mouth and accepted the rubber ball gag as he pulled it tight behind my head and fastened it.

Conner put his right hand on my back and held me against the dresser while he reached under my dress with his other hand. Pulling down my panties, he checked my hole and found the plug he placed there over a month earlier.
"Good girl, you left it in." He said.

I moaned as he began tugging at the plug. After staying in for several hours, my hole had tightened around it once again. My hole stretched as Conner pulled the plug out ever so slowly. I moaned through the gag as the widest part reached the opening and popped out. Although the pressure was released, I had become so accustomed to the feeling of the plug inside of me that I felt empty without it. I continued moaning as I waited for what was to come.

Conner unzipped his pants and pulled down his underwear before bringing his middle to my behind. I couldn't believe how large he was as he slid between my cheeks and kept pushing forward. The plug started thin and worked its way up to the widest part, but this was entirely different. His head pushed forward against my opening and continued applying pressure until it was accepted.

Despite being plugged constantly for the last month, I could feel myself stretching considerably to make room for Conner's head. I moaned and whimpered in my gag as Conner slowly pushed himself forward until he was all the way inside. My legs felt weak as he pressed me against the dresser with me bent over it.

I squealed as the base of his middle met my cheeks and paused for a moment. I pulled my head back and let out a muffled moan as he began sliding himself back out of me. I literally could not believe how much larger he was than the dildo or the plug. From the pressure in my hole, it felt like he was twice as large as the butt plug that he had stuck inside of me. After pulling all the way out, he moved back forward and pressed all the way back in again. I thumped against the dresser while my boobs bounced back and forth. Without a bra on, my breasts began bouncing with the rhythm of Conner's thrusts.

My focus began shifting between my E cup breasts and the rod penetrating me from behind. I squealed through the gag as I felt Conner moving faster and faster behind me, knocking me against the dresser as he did. I continued moaning as my breasts bounced back and forth in sync with Conner. Although I felt incredibly sexy for Conner, I began wishing I put on a bra to hold everything in place. As Conner continued speeding up, I felt familiar sensations building in my behind and working their way to my middle.

After having been locked up for over a month, my middle had grown accustomed to the cage. My middle had given up on trying to grow and felt like it even shrank slightly. As my member sat comfortably in its cage, I began feeling a release approaching.

I let out muffled screams into the gag as Conner slapped my ass. I could feel every vain from his member as he tensed up inside of me. Conner grabbed my hair and yanked it backwards as he began moving as fast as he could. He was in complete control of my body as it bounced between his pelvis and the dresser. As I heard moaning begin to escape Conner, I knew the end was imminent.

I moaned with Conner as I felt my own climax within reach. As Conner continued pumping behind me, small drops of liquid began dribbling from my cage. Conner began slowing down his thrusts as I felt warm liquid rushing into my behind. I squealed through the gag as this new feeling swept me away. The warm sensations were enough to push me over the edge as Conner continued slowly but roughly plunging into me.

My trapped member began leaking and oozing out liquid in sync with Conner. With each thrust from Conner, each of us oozed out a little more. I felt a wave come over me as we both emptied ourselves of everything that had built up. Once the squirts ceased, he slowed himself to a stop and pulled himself out. I stood bent over the dresser breathing heavily as I came down from one of the most intense orgasms of my life.

Conner let go of my hair and backed away as I stood ready for more. He grabbed the plug and guided it back into my behind. After experiencing all of Conner, the plug felt tiny in comparison. I felt like the plug could drop right out before Conner pulled up my panties and pulled down my dress.

Conner released me from my handcuffs and gag before slapping my behind and ordering me back to my room. I followed Conner's orders and made my way back to bed. After resting my head for a few minutes, I was fast asleep.

CHAPTER 14

I had the best night sleep since I arrived at Conner's penthouse. I awoke the next morning feeling completely refreshed and brand new as the sun shined through the windows. Jumping out of bed, I raced through my morning routine with excitement as I couldn't wait to see Conner again.

I raced over to the door after hearing a knock. The butler was standing in front of me with my smoothie and pills as usual.
"Oh thank you." I said as I grabbed my breakfast and began gulping it down. "What is Conner doing today?"
"He left early this morning, but he said that he will be back late next week."
My stomach dropped as I heard the news. "He left again?"
"Yes madam. I am also supposed to inform you that you have another appointment with Doctor Bentenhousen today after your appointment at the salon."
"Again? I was just at the Doctor a week ago."
"Yes madam. You must be ready soon, the driver will be here shortly."
"Ok, I'll get ready and do my makeup."
"That will not be necessary madam. Just get dressed and come with me downstairs right away."
"Ok?" I said as I closed the door and walked over to the closet.

I found a simple black knee length skirt and blue blouse that I paired with black high heel pumps. After getting dressed quickly, I walked back over to the door to find the butler still waiting.
"Ready madam?"
"I guess so."
The butler escorted me down to the main entranceway before I walked outside and found the driver. He smiled as he held the door open for me. I took his hand and stepped into the vehicle.

After a short ride across the city, we arrived at the salon. The driver opened my door and helped me out before I walked up. Jessica was waiting

at the front and greeted me before walking me to the back room.
"Hey hunny, how are you doing today?" Jessica asked.
"Good I guess." I answered.
"Oh what's the matter." Jessica asked as she sat me down in the chair.
"Well, Conner has been away a lot lately and he just got back last night, then left again. I guess he's going to be away another week or something?"
"Oh, I'm sorry sweetie. Have you two spent any quality time together?" Jessica said as she began touching up my fingernails. After a month, my nails began to grow out and show my nail beds.
"Well last night he surprised me in bed when he got home. He made me feel like the only girl in the world. It was so romantic, we both finished at the same time and then the night ended."
"That sounds lovely dear. So what's the matter?"
"Well I woke up this morning and found out that he had to leave before I woke up."
"Are you upset he didn't say goodbye?"
"Well yeah kinda. I just don't like that he has to leave so much."
"I'm sorry dear. But do you know who needs to hear this?"
"Who?" I said while looking at Jessica through the mirror.
"Conner." She said as she looked into my eyes.
"I guess your right."
"I know I am girl. Now what do you think?" Jessica asked after finishing up my nails.
I held my hands in front of me and took in the long red nails. "They're beautiful!"
"Thanks girl. I guess this was all for today." Jessica said as she stood behind me. "I really hope everything works out with you and Conner. If any girl can tame him, it would be a sweetie like you."
"What do you mean?" I asked.
"Well I didn't think it was a secret that Mr. Wellington has been with a lot of girls."
"Like how many?"
"It's hard to say?" Jessica said.
"But if you had to guess."
"Well, I've been working here for the last ten years and have seen at least a dozen girls come through."

"And what happened to them?" I asked feeling concerned.

"I really don't know dear. All I can tell you is, once they have boobs the size of yours, it's typically their last appointment."

I sat in the chair stunned at what Jessica was sharing with me.

"Don't worry dear, none of the other girls were as sweet as you. I'm sure everything will be alright." Jessica added.

"Thank you Jessica, you are a real friend."

"Thank you sweetie."

I sat up from my chair and gave Jessica a hug before leaving.

As I made my way back to the limousine and met the driver out front, I couldn't help but shed a tear. Jessica was the only person I felt like I could share my life with. I just hoped that this wouldn't be the last time we were together.

I stared out the window as the driver brought me to my next appointment. I felt anxiety creeping up as we arrived. The driver opened my door and helped me out. I took a deep breath before walking up to the building and making my way to Doctor Bentenhousen's office.

The nurse greeted me and walked me back to the operating room. I sat nervously in the chair as I awaited the doctor.

"Hello, how are we doing today?" He asked.

"I'm good." I answered.

"Very good. If you don't have any questions, we can go ahead and get started."

"What exactly are we doing today?"

"Oh, I thought you had been filled in already. Your staff called and said you wanted to move up your appointments. Today you are scheduled to have a full facial reconstruction. We are going to work on your nose, cheek bones, chin and neck to make them smoother and more feminine. Then, we will finish up by plumping those lips up nice and full."

"Are there any other surgeries scheduled?"

"We will have a few more checkups but that will be the extent of what's left."

I took a deep breath as I sat in the chair. "Ok, thank you doctor."

"No problem, I will be right back and we'll get started."

CHAPTER 15

I awoke the next day back in my bed in Conner's penthouse. I must have been put out deeper and longer as I felt even more groggy than the first surgery. My eyes fluttered open as I struggled to lift my head from its pillow. I let out a loud moan as I struggled to sit up in my bed.

I heard footsteps in the hallway before the butler appeared shortly after.

"Hello madam, how are you feeling?" He asked.

"Terrible." I answered.

"I am sorry madam, they said it could be rough the first few days, but you will recover in about a week."

I lifted my hand up to my face and began prodding at the bandages wrapped around my head.

"Please don't do that madam, they said it needs to remain covered and undisturbed while you heal."

"It itches so bad."

"Here take this." The butler said holding out a couple of blue pills and water. "It will help with the pain."

I took the pills from his hand and struggled to swallow them with water.

"I will leave you to rest a while. Let me know if you need anything."

I closed my eyes and drifted back to sleep before the butler left.

The next few days felt like a dreamlike state as I drifted in and out of sleep. The butler would awaken me for my pain medication, hormones, and meals, but otherwise left me to rest. By the fifth day of my recovery, I finally started to feel somewhat normal again.

The last two days of wearing the bandages around my whole head felt twice as long as the first five. I did my best to stay in bed and not touch my face, but the itching was becoming unbearable. After the longest week of my life, I laid my head down for the last night before I could remove the bandage wrap.

I barely slept through the night as I tossed and turned constantly. My eyes were wide open before the sun came up and shined through my window. I jumped out of bed and eagerly awaited the butler. After a few minutes, he knocked on my door.

"Are you ready madam."

"Just get this off of me already." I demanded.

The butler walked over to me and began carefully removing the wrap. As layer after layer peeled off, I tapped my toes on the floor next to the bed. I appreciated that he was being carful, but I was losing my patience.

"Almost there." He said as he came down around my chin.

At last, the final piece of wrap was gone. The butler stepped back as I raced over to the bathroom and inspected myself.

I was dumbfounded as I stared at the reflection in the mirror. Everything about my face that was even remotely male was now gone. My nose appeared tiny and cute while my cheek bones looked higher and well defined. My chin looked sharper and thinner and my lips were luscious and full. My adam's apple had completely disappeared along with my male identity. Even without makeup, everything about my head was feminine, delicate, and beautiful.

I stood up straight and brought my hands underneath my breasts as I took in my whole reflection. My red painted fingers caressed my round, full E cup breasts that were pushed up by a hot pink bra. I ran them down the bottom of my cups, past my ribs, and around my waist. I brought my fingers around my waist and managed to touch the nails of my thumb and middle fingers together.

My fingers kept wandering south as they moved down to my middle and slid under my lace pink panties. The only thing still marking me as a male was in the palm of my hands. I ran my fingers around the cage and prodded it with my finger. I twitched in my cage as I felt my fingernail poke through.

The cage had felt incredibly tight when it was first locked on me almost two months ago. Now after two months of being unable to grow erect, I wondered if I even could anymore. I pulled my hands out of my panties and fixed my bra before walking back out to the bedroom.

The butler was standing with my smoothie and pills in hand. After guzzling my breakfast, I handed the butler back the glass.

"Will you be needing anything else madam?"

"Will Conner still be returning tonight?" I asked.

"He will be arriving just before dinner tonight."

"Thank you."

"My pleasure madam." He said as he stepped out and closed the door.

Feeling excited and worried to see Conner, I walked into the bathroom to begin getting myself ready. After my conversation with Jessica, I wanted to do everything I could to make this evening perfect. I hadn't seen Conner much since I started living with him and was determined to make myself look perfect.

I stood in front of the mirror and took in the image staring back at me. With the work that had been done by Dr. Bentenhousen, as well as my strict dieting and hormones, my face had never looked better. I grabbed my foundation and began applying a thing layer to make sure my skin looked even. Once I was finished with the liquid foundation, I grabbed the setting powder and applied a fine layer before moving on to my blush.

While sweeping the blush across my cheekbones, I came to realize that less would be more. Having been a crossdresser for years, I typically layered my makeup heavily and did everything I could to disguise my male features. However, having just reconstructed my face, it didn't need any contouring or anything more than a little foundation and a touch of blush. After a few smooth strokes of the blush, I set down the powder and moved on to the eye brow pencil.

I found it easier to keep my eyebrows plucked to the point of non existence and rely more heavily on my brow pencil. While drawing on two matching thin eye brows, I leaned in close to the mirror and kept a close eye. Once I felt that they were perfect, I moved on to my eyes.

Using dark eye shadow, I created a smokey eye look. Carefully guiding the eyeliner around each eye, I circled my eyes and finished with a small wing. I grabbed the lash volume mascara and began applying it generously to my lashes. Although I felt like I didn't need much makeup in other areas, I absolutely loved the feeling of long, full eyelashes.

After finishing up my eyes, I drew my attention toward my lips. I carefully outlined my cupid's arrow with a dark red lip liner before filling in the rest of my lips with a matching dark red lip stain. Applying a top layer of shiny lip gloss, I puckered my lips and blew a kiss to the mirror.

Once I was finished with my makeup, I walked over to my dresser and opened the top drawer. Grabbing a matching pair of black lace panties and bra, I began sliding up the panties over my locked middle. My middle flinched as it felt the lace panties rub against it through the cage. I shuttered before pulling my strapless bra around me and fastening it.

I arched my back as I stood in front of the mirror hanging on the closet door. Bringing my hands up to my chest, I adjusted my boobs and made sure that they looked even. I couldn't help but let out a giggle as I handled my very own pair of E cup breasts.

I walked into the closet and began scanning for the sexiest piece of clothing I could find. My eyes glanced over silky dresses, ball gowns, and other elegant outfits. As I made my way to the back of the closet, I discovered a dress that I hadn't seen before. Hanging in-between a few other black dresses was a short form fitting black latex dress. I pulled it from the hanger and held it in my hand.
'This will definitely get his attention.' I thought to myself.

I stepped into the dress and pulled it up my body. The dress didn't have any zippers but was held in place by how tightly it fit. I pulled the strapless dress over my chest and adjusted it to make sure my boobs looked right. I gave a light tug at the bottom of the dress to straighten it out before stepping over to the mirror again.

The black latex dress looked like it melded with my skin as it accentuated every curvature of my body. Coming down just passed my butt, it barely left anything for the imagination. I turned to my side as I took in the fullness of my breasts underneath the form fitting material. The top of the dress held tightly just above my breasts as it had no straps holding it up.

I walked back to the closet and searched in the shoe holes for something to match the appeal of my dress. Sitting in one of the shoe holes on the floor, I noticed a pair of knee high leather high heel boots. I pulled them from their hole and sat on the bed before I slid my feet inside.

As I slid the zipper up the leather material, my legs were encased from toes to knees. The boots form fitted around my calves and left no opening at the top of the boot. As I stood, I could feel just how high the five and a half inch high heel boots were without any platform to help. I walked in front of the mirror and took another look at myself.

Between the makeup, the fiery red hair, the tight fitting dress, and the outrageously high heel boots, I never looked sexier in my life. If Conner wasn't impressed by me tonight, I didn't know if I could ever do enough for him. Although my hair was still holding its style from the previous day, I decided to work on it while I had time.

After an hour of styling and working on my hair, I walked over to my windows and watched over the city. As the afternoon sun began to descend, I was becoming nervous about my dinner with Conner.
'I feel like I've barely even seen him since I've been here. He's been kind of sweet but really short with me, I just hope he thinks I look sexy tonight. I mean, he has fucked me a few times now, so he must think I'm kind of sexy? I just hope he doesn't dump me or get rid of me like Jessica said he does with everyone else.'

Eventually, the sun fell behind the buildings and dinner was imminent. I felt butterflies fluttering in my stomach as the butler's footsteps approached my room. I stayed sitting on my bed as the butler opened the door.
"Are you ready for dinner madam?" He asked.
"Yes thank you." I answered.
I followed behind the butler as we walked to the dining room. I jumped as I stepped through the doorway and saw Conner sitting at the table.
"Conner." I said reactively.
Conner turned his attention from his phone to me as he sat at his seat. I was expecting to sit and wait for him as usual, but he had beaten me here tonight.
"Well, you look lovely tonight." Conner said. "Come, sit down."
I nervously walked over to my seat next to Conner with my hands together in front of me. The butler walked behind me and pulled out my seat for me to sit.
"Thank you." I said to the butler.
"It's my pleasure madam." He answered.
Conner gave a nod to the butler and he was off to the kitchen.
"So, how have you been enjoying your time here so far?" Conner asked.
"It's been lovely, I just wish I could see more of you." I answered.
"I have been gone a lot haven't I?"
"Yeah, I feel like I barely get to see you. I mean, I love the sex, its like super hot, but I want to get to know you better, you know?"
"I don't know if you know what your asking."

"What do you mean?"
"Do you know where I spend most of my time?"
"I wish you would tell me."
"In the Caribbean."
"Oh, ok?"
"I own a small island down there that I visit frequently with guests. When I'm not here or at my place in Paris, I like to spend most of my time there with my girls."
"Your girls?" I asked. "So you've been in the Caribbean with other girls this whole time?"
"Not the whole time, but most of it. See, when I meet someone special, I like to have them stay with me while my butler keeps an eye on them. If they are willing to do what I ask and listen to what they are told, I like to invite them to come live in my Caribbean community."

My face was a mixture of shock and curiosity as the butler walked in with our meals. The butler had skipped the salads tonight and slid a plate of fresh fish in front of Conner and myself. The fish appeared white and flaky and was prepared with a teriyaki glaze. Each plate was paired with some fresh greens and a small amount of risotto.
"You can eat like this every night, spend as much time with me as you like, and live in the Caribbean. All you have to do is say yes." Conner said with a fork and knife in hand.
"That sounds great. It really does, but would I be able to come back?" I asked.
"Eventually, but we like to stay together as a tight knit community down there. Trust me, once you come down, you won't want to leave."
"Who are the other girls though?"
"They were just like you. They were people who didn't have a lot of luck in their male life and wanted something new and exciting. I helped them reach their full potential and now I take care of anything they need."
"I really don't know what to say."
"All I need to hear is your answer."
"My answer?"
"Yes, what will it be?" Conner asked while looked deep into my eyes.
My heart was pounding as I looked down at my plate. Conner had already devoured most of his food in-between sentences and was now waiting for me. I swallowed the excess saliva in my mouth and looked back into Con-

ner's blue eyes.

"I would love to spend more time with you and live with you in the Caribbean." I said with a smile.

Conner smiled back and extended his hand toward me. I accepted his hand as he stood up and guided me out of the dining room. I hadn't even started my meal, but that was the last thing on my mind. Conner led me down the hall to his favorite room before shutting the door behind us. I had no idea what was in store for me or my future, but with Conner by my side, I was ready for anything.

EPILOGUE

My mouth was watering as we entered Conner's special room. I had no idea what it would be, but I knew something would be entering my mouth soon. Conner left me by the door and walked over to the dresser. Pulling something out, he held it behind his back as he walked over to me.
"Turn around." He ordered.
I did as he said and faced the closed door.

Conner grabbed my wrists and slid a pair of hand cuffs around them. The leather hand cuffs had fur on the inside and felt comfortable to the wrists. He pulled them tightly around each wrist and locked them on with a padlock. Holding on to a long leather strap attached the handcuffs, he pulled my wrists up to my mid back and held them there.

Conner slid a rubber ball gag around my head and pulled the ball into my mouth. I opened my mouth as I accepted the gag. As he pulled the strap tight behind my head and locked it, I could feel that the ball gag and my hand cuffs were attached by the leather strap behind me. My wrists hung around my mid to lower back as they pulled on the gag buried in my mouth. The harder I pulled on my cuffs, the tighter the gag was pulled into my mouth. I found it easiest to let my arms rest with minimal pressure to my gag.

Conner walked back over to the dresser and returned with a leather collar and leash. I stood still as he pulled the collar around my neck and locked it snugly in place. It did not restrict breathing but I was definitely aware of its presence. He attached the leash to my collar and smiled.

Conner lead me by the leash over to the corner with the cage. He rolled the cage away from the wall so that there was room to walk around it before ordering me inside.
"Go on, I know you can crawl in." He said.
In my high heels and tight dress, I wasn't as sure as Conner. I followed his order anyway and struggled to go down on my knees. Conner held the leash tight as I put one knee down first, then the other. I brought my head down

and scooted on my knees inside of the cage.

The steel cage was just large enough for one person to fit inside. It had steel bars around the entire exterior along with a door on one end and a small hatch on the other. I struggled as I scooted on the plastic tray floor inside of the cage and turned myself around to face the open door. Conner knelt down in front of the door and pulled the leash down toward the ground. As I sat on my knees, my head came down to the floor of the cage and hovered just above. Conner ran the leash around the left side of the cage before bringing it around the right side as well. He tied the leash off beneath my neck which held my head inches from the cage floor. Conner closed the cage door and locked it shut.

I was starting to get nervous as Conner had previously not gone to such great lengths to confine me. I wasn't claustrophobic, but I was starting to wonder when the sex would begin. I shifted my behind as Conner stood up and walked behind me. I heard a rattling on the back of the cage as Conner opened up a small hatch. He reached inside of the cage and pulled my behind up toward the opening. I moaned as I had to strain to keep my butt positioned in front of the opening.

Conner unzipped himself and pulled out his member behind me. I could feel as he pulled down my panties and exposed my rear. His fingers reached between my cheeks and pulled out the plug still in place. I moaned as my opening stretched to release the flared object. Conner pinched my cheek before plunging himself straight ahead.

I screamed through the gag as Conner wasted no time forcing his way all the way inside of me. Although I had been wearing a plug for some time now, it still felt like I needed to warm up. Conner held himself all the way inside for a few moments before slowly pulling himself all the way out. I began breathing heavily as Conner pushed forward and entered me again.

While I laid in the cage, my breasts pressed against the floor beneath me. As Conner began moving back and forth behind me, I began rocking back and forth inside of the cage. I felt a tingling in my nipples as they rubbed back and forth on the cage floor to the rhythm of Conner's thrusts. As the sensations grew, my moaning grew as well.

Conner began pumping back and forth harder as I struggled to press my bottom against the back wall of the cage. I strained against my cuffs as I felt an orgasm building inside of me. Hearing the heavy breathing from

Conner, I knew that he was as close as I was. I began whimpering as the sensations in my chest and behind were competing for my attention.

I had never experienced as strong of feelings as the ones Conner was giving me. I pulled at my collar and kicked the back of my cage as I felt like I couldn't possibly take anymore. I was so close to a climax I felt like I could taste it. I screamed through my gag as Conner gave his hardest thrusts.

Conner was in complete and total control of me as he finally blew his load. I could feel him slowing down as squirts of warm liquid rushed inside of me. I held my behind to the cage and tried bouncing up and down for him to continue, but he was clearly finished. I whimpered through the gag as Conner pulled out and zipped his pants back up. I continued moaning and whining as Conner grabbed the plug and inserted it back inside of me. After pulling up my panties, he closed the hatch to the cage.

Walking back around to the front of the cage, Conner knelt down to my level. I strained to look up into his deep, blue eyes.
"I hope that was as incredible for you as it was for me." Conner said.
I moaned through the gag, begging him for more.
"Don't worry, after the flight, we'll have plenty of time to do this again."
I swallowed my saliva as I continued staring up at Conner.
"Just stay put while I let the butler know you're ready for shipment. I am so happy you decided to do this. You will not regret it."
My eyes went wide as I watched Conner walk out. I screamed through the gag as he shut the door and left me alone in the dimly lit room. All I could think about as I laid in my cage was whether or not I made yet another mistake in my dating life.

BOOKS BY THIS AUTHOR

Maid To Be Mine

Have you dreamt of becoming a sissy maid for a dominating woman? Have you wondered how a man can go from a couch potato to the sissy maid everyone wants in their house?
Maid to be mine explores the sissy maid lifestyle from the perspective of a woman who is learning about it for the first time. After her boyfriend tells her about his little secret, she decides to give the female led relationship a try. She quickly learns how exciting and empowering it is to have a sissy maid that cooks, cleans, and does anything she asks. Having your own sissy maid doesn't come easy though, she learns that the secret to controlling your sissy is with chastity and complete control of his body. Once he is locked away, he will do anything for one more release. Watch as this sissy learns that sissies are maid to be shared. Join this sissy as they find out just how hard it can be to serve their masters.

Cat And Mouse

What happens when you lock two sissies in a room together and shut off the lights? How would you react to a mob boss's daughter taking you under her wing and turning you into her personal play doll?

Let me introduce you to the next title in forced feminization stories 'Cat and Mouse.' Bona is down on his luck and has just been accused of being a rat against his mob family. Before he is "disposed of", he is taken under the wing of the mob boss's daughter. He loses all control of his body and his will as Elaina turns Bona into her little sissy play toy. Little does Bona know, he is not the only play toy that she owns. Bona has to learn to get along with his new roommate and potential lover as he is tied up and completely feminized. Follow the story as Bona is trained by this 19 year old girl and is completely humiliated in front of his old co workers and boss. Forced to wear the highest of ballet heels, Latex dresses, Makeup, collar and leash, this sissy is going to have to learn what it means to be Elaina's little sissy toy. When it comes to altering this sissy's body and chest, nothing is off the table for Elaina. Will our sissy learn to accept their role and listen to what they're told, or will they try to fight and run away?

Past The Point Of No Return

Have you ever wondered what it would be like to be a sissy slut? Have you ever fantasized about dressing up as a sissy maid, doing your make up, wearing a wig, and high heels? Have you thought about meeting someone who would tie you up and do what they wanted with you?
In Past the Point of No Return, the main character finds out exactly what it is like to be tied up and

completely changed into a feminized sissy slut. Our protagonist makes the mistake of responding to a phishing email from a mysterious dominatrix. After meeting up and letting his guard down, he finds out that he can never go back to his old life again. He will now be made to wear the highest of heels, stockings, matching pink panties and bra, and form fitting latex dresses for the rest of his life. As the sissy progresses, he is hypnotized by his masters until he becomes a full fledged sissy bimbo that obeys every command. The story explores Forced feminization, Feminization surgery, Bimbofication, sissy hypnotism, sissy prostitution, bondage, and much more. If you are still reading this and haven't been scared off, this may be the book for you.

My Body Swap With Candi

Have you ever wondered what it would be like to swap bodies with an escort for a week? Have you wondered what it would be like to leave your male body behind and inhabit a sensual and sexy woman's body?

In 'My Body Swap with Candi', our stubborn protagonist meets up with an escort at a motel. After visiting the motel numerous times and having plenty of 'sessions' with different ladies, he meets a very special lady named Candi. As he is 'getting to know' Candi, our protagonist starts to learn that this is no ordinary girl. He believes she is becoming delirious as they make love in her room. After they finish their session, he realizes that he has made a huge mistake and tries to escape. While trying to process what just happened, the protagonist receives a phone call that will change his life. As the story unfolds, our protagonist learns that he has fallen into a situation more complex than he could possibly imagine. The protagonist's consciousness is placed into Candi's body while her consciousness inhabits his body. He must learn to follow the rules and live out Candi's life while fulfilling her duties. Will he do as he is told and return to his male body, or be stuck as Candi forever?

Becoming The Girl Of His Dreams

Have you ever had sissy dreams when you fell asleep? Have you ever wished that those dreams of crossdressing, wearing makeup, and walking around in high heels would come true?
When a young man who is hiding the sissy inside has a strange encounter, he is told that all of his dreams will start to come true. After falling asleep and dreaming of having his nails done and painted bright pink, he wakes up to discover that his nails have become bright pink and painted in real life. When he dreams of having a large set of boobs, the dream manifests before his eyes. As the story progresses, the dreams completely feminize the young man until he is no longer recognizable as one. Unable to process the changes in his fragile male psyche, he denies what is happening and tries to fight back against his female dominator. Will the sissy convince her dominatrix to reverse the changes that are happening or will the sissy have to learn how to live as the woman that they have always dreamt of being?

Made in United States
Orlando, FL
30 July 2023